"Rikki Ducornet's [*Phosphor* _____ _____ _____ _l-binding masterpiece. The exercise of her extravagant imaginative powers is rigorous, the richness of her writing concentrated to trenchant effect, and her enchanting narrative conducted with great intensity and seriousness. Phosphor's bewildering, bewildered career deserves a constellation in the firmament of literary heroes."—**Harry Mathews**

"Like all her work it is astonishing; a breathtaking succession of marvels—its fertility and wit are staggering."—**Robert Harbison**

"Rikki Ducornet can create an unsettling, dreamlike beauty out of any subject. In the heady mix of her fiction, everything becomes potently suggestive, resonant, fascinating. She exposes life's harshest truths with a mesmeric delicacy and holds her readers spellbound."—**Joanna Scott**

"Ducornet is a novelist of ambition and scope."—*The New York Times*

"Linguistically explosive. . . . One of the most interesting American writers around."—*The Nation*

"Pick up a book by the award-winning Ducornet, and you know it will be startling, elegant, and perfectly formed."—*Library Journal*

"Storytelling that enchants the senses."—*The Boston Globe*

"Ducornet is a writer of extraordinary power, in whose books 'rigor and imagination' (her watchwords) perform with the grace and daring of high-wire acrobats." —*BOMB*

"Ducornet's is a world of surfaces so rich and textured that notions of meaning and interpretation are subsumed under a lush and seductive prose that eventually inhabits readers' minds."—*The Millions*

"[R]eveals strangeness in the most basic circumstances of life, flooding them in new light."—*Kenyon Review*

"Ducornet is a mad maestro of words."—*Seattle Weekly*

"Writer, poet, and artist Ducornet does things with words most authors would never even dream of."—**Men's Journal**

"Rikki Ducornet is a magic sensualist, a writer's writer, a master of language, a unique voice."—**Amy Tan**

"It is Rikki Ducornet's magic to be able to coax an entire universe--'restless beyond imagining, a universe of rock and flame, whose nature is incandescence'--out of the modest and often grim contours of one man's life."—**Kathryn Davis**

"*Netsuke* comes at the summit of Rikki Ducornet's passionate, caring, and accomplished career. Its readers will pick up pages of painful beauty and calamitous memory, and their focus will be like a burning glass; its examination of a ruinous sexual life is as delicate and sharp as a surgeon's knife. And the rendering? The rendering is as good as it gets."—**William Gass**

"One of America's most incandescent satiric writers. . . . *Phosphor in Dreamland* has much to impart about European Expansionism, its brutal vanities, religious persecution and the scourge of one culture"s fear and ultimate hatred of the erotic, the natural , the mysterious . . ."—*The LA Times*

OTHER BOOKS BY RIKKI DUCORNET

NOVELS

The Stain
Entering Fire
The Fountains of Neptune
The Jade Cabinet
Trafik
Brightfellow
Netsuke
Gazelle
The Fan Maker's Inquisition

SHORT FICTION

The Complete Butcher's Tales
The Plotinus (novella)
The One Marvelous Thing
The Word Desire

POETRY

From the Star Chamber
Wild Geraniums
Weird Sisters
Knife Notebook
The Illustrated Universe
The Cult of Seizure

ESSAYS

The Monstrous and the Marvelous
The Deep Zoo

Rikki Ducornet

PHOSPHOR IN DREAMLAND

DALKEY ARCHIVE PRESS

Dallas / Dublin

First edition 1995
First Dalkey Archive Essentials edition, 2023
Published by arrangement with Agence littéraire Astier-Pécher
Portions of this novel first appeared in *Black Ice, Fiction International, Iowa Review, New Observations, Parnassus, Postmodern Culture*, and *Sulphur.*

The author wishes to extend her thanks to Allan Guttmann and the Copeland Colloquium Sponsors at Amherst College, Jeanie Kim and Patrick Lannan of the Lannan Foundation, Giovanna Covi and the University of Trento, and John O'Brien and Steven Moore of Dalkey Archive Press.

Ebook: 978-1-62897-470-6

Library of Congress Cataloging-in-Publication Data Ducornet, Rikki, 1943-Phosphor in dreamland / Rikki Ducornet. — 1st ed. p. cm.

I. Title.
PS3554.U279P48 1995   813'.54—dc20   95-17888
ISBN 1-56478-084-8

Partially funded by grants from the National Endowment for the Arts and the Illinois Arts Council.

Cover design by Justin Childress
Interior design by Anuj Mathur

Dalkey Archive Press
www.dalkeyarchive.com
Dallas/Dublin

Printed on permanent/durable acid-free paper.

For Jonathan: these instants

. . . into the virgin forest,
Thicket of wild things, went the men, and down . . .

—Virgil, *The Aeneid* (trans. Robert Fitzgerald)

PROLOGUE

My beloved friend V. S. Krishnamurti—

The small scientific community here is grateful—and always will be—for your delightful histories of amorous bivalves, and your descriptions of Argonauta gamboling upon the placid waters of Turtle Soup Bay beneath the moon. Often I recall those marvelous conversations we had years ago during your last visit here; recall your conceit that all living things carry fables—the fabulous histories of their being within their cells: each creature an encyclopedia written in code. You likened the chromosomes to the Minotaur's maze, the face of the Medusa, a map of Milano, Mars seen from space. And now, having reread this little history of Birdland in which language plays a major part, I cannot help but remember, dearest Ved, how you would toss morsels of Sanskrit at me and scraps of Tantric lore, and profoundly engage me—just as once I saw you engage a dolphin by tossing it an armful of fish.

Because I know that you are always eager to learn more about this place which has been my home since boyhood and which has, to my delight, excited your curiosity on the rare occasions of your eagerly awaited visits from your all-too-distant Australia, I have taken the liberty to dedicate this brief history of Birdland to you (or, more precisely, this *revery*).

If most of what is related here happened over three hundred years ago and reads like a romance, you know me well enough to trust this account has been carefully documented. I have read each word on the subject of this my fragile, my startling island still so rich in rarities (and I am thinking of those albino bivalves you discovered, the scarlet bottom-feeding rays).

I have held every artifact kept within our beautiful coral-walled museum and read every book in the library; I have, with binoculars, explored on foot the island's entire length and breadth, my sleepless nights punctuated by the sound of gastropods noisily snapping shut their valves. And although I know it is impossible, even now I pray that by some miracle, as I sit in silence on a lump of volcanic glass off the leeward coast, I shall hear the lôplôp singing, or smell the sacred smoke of an aboriginal shaman's cigar. So much has vanished!

Ironically, the greatest boon to my project has been the discovery of Rais Secundo's inquiry—which had slept for three centuries in a broom closet. If the Inquisitor was responsible for the destruction of Nuño Alfa y Omega's magnificent opus (as well as countless ocularscopic plates), much has been preserved within the inquiry itself.

Secundo's need to justify his acts of vandalism—if only to himself—constrained him to keep examples of what he sought to suppress and so, despite himself, assure the survival of some of the world's most astonishing erotica.

True, the *intention* of the ocularscopic project, funded by

Fantasma, was not only *magical* but *pornographic*. However, Nuño Alfa y Omega was not only an inventor of precocious genius, but a great artist, and the results—those lascivious nudes and multifarious copulations—can only be called transcendent.

Recently an insular group has attempted, once again, to suppress those incandescent verses and consign the ocularscopic plates to oblivion. Even before my little book has seen the light of day, it is the cause of a heated controversy. I was present the morning the "Clean Sweepers" stormed the museum carrying hammers and brooms with the intent to smash those unique artifacts you have so admired. In the scuffle, the mysteriously beautiful *Ama-ma-mu*—the jewel of the collection—was dashed to the floor. But that obsidian Venus, copulating so freely with a lôplôp on her molluscan couch, proved tougher than parquet. She has been returned unscathed to her niche, and the fine extracted from the "Clean Sweepers" has purchased an electronic eye. As tireless as an angel, it watches over her night and day.

1

Several hundred years ago, the mendicant scholar Fogginius was roused from the depths of nightmare by a hellish bawling.

Fogginius leapt up from his bed—in truth a worn, woolen cape sewn into a sack and stuffed with shredded shirts—and threw aside his door, or rather, the crusted board which kept the wild hogs from relieving themselves in his rooms. There, upon the overturned kettle he used as a threshold, lay an abandoned human infant, soiled, club-footed, and with crossed eyes.

Fogginius washed it, stared fiercely into its transverse gaze, and in the manner of the times swaddled it so tightly that it could not thrash but only howl—as helpless as a sausage damned with a thwarted consciousness. This done, he christened it Nuño Alfa y Omega. But because of the infant's apparent *luminosity*, he called it *Phosphor*.

Fogginius was disliked. A deaf man, whom the scholar had cured of a coughing fit by stuffing his ears with breadcrumbs and parsley, daily damned him; another, whose beehives Fogginius had smeared with dung, hated and feared him.

Nevertheless, up until the arrival of Professor Tardanza from Cordova, and Phosphor's maturity, he was the only scholar in Birdland, and his the island's only library—a wormy collection of books stuffing a trunk not large enough to bathe in. The books had been packed along with that woolen cape and those nightshirts which, a full three decades later, served the saint as mattress.

In his youth, Fogginius had been enthralled by Birdland's unique bestiary. The island claimed a feathered serpent, a voiceless dog, a silent cat, and large albino spiders sporting pink bristles. After many years of trial and error, he had taught himself the ambiguous art of taxidermy and so was able to save the skins of almost anything he chose, although he was not an artist and was incapable of reconstructing any creature convincingly. For example, Fogginius' snakes did not diminish towards the tail, but instead—as a specimen on display in the municipal museum demonstrates—grew progressively fatter.

So zealous was the scholar and so thorough that all the living creatures within three kilometers of his hovel had utterly vanished by the time my story begins. Only their skins remained—thousands upon thousands of them—decomposing in sisal sacks and crowding the shadows of the room Fogginius used as library, laboratory, kitchen, and bed chamber, and which the rats used as a larder. He saw to his personal needs after dark beside the path that led to a little chapel—no more in his keeping (for word of other excesses had reached his queen). Because Fogginius cured his skins with grease, the salted livers of voles, the ashes of wild hog testicles, and vinegar, his place and person smelled unlike any other. And once, perhaps in jest, perhaps the result of rare and hermetic readings, Fogginius had suggested that the Savior was a false prophet, a magician engendered by the planet Mars. He was fortunate to have escaped with his life. A new priest—Fogginius despised him—was sent to oversee the cosmic affairs of Birdland.

❧

The city in which Fogginius lived had been named Pope Publius by a bishop in absentia. As may still be seen in the Old Quarter, its houses were of local pudding stone and coral, and, at the time of this history, well over a century old. Each had been fitted with heavy doors, high balconies, and iron-barred windows—for in its early years the island had been plagued by pirates. The shops—generously fitted with closets, storage bins, and shelvings—were for the most part empty of everything but lizards. If Pope Publius had been prosperous for several decades, it was no longer—although one rich man remained in the city's finest house, its spiral stairs listing and its mahogany columns riddled by carpenter ants. The walls were imported marble, and the windows of Venetian glass.

This palace belonged to Señor Fango Fantasma, that same Fantasma whose grandfather had been among the first to take possession of the island. Now that his inherited wealth was running out, Señor Fantasma was waiting for a shipload of Africans—for whom he had negotiated with the papal authorities for nearly a decade—to work in mines that he feared the atomized aborigines had already scraped to the bone. And there were plantations, too: of pineapple and cinnamon and cassia. Once as ordered as formal gardens, these, for lack of upkeep, had been, in great part, reclaimed by the encroaching jungle.

Very little is known about the original population of
Birdland—only that it venerated the cigar and dwelt in great
baskets. As the climate of the island is extremely mild, the
natives had no need of smokeholes. They cooked their meals
outside in a common courtyard fenced in by the shells of
outsized clams. The small hole at the top of their huts was
the eye by which they could be perceived by curiously indel-
icate gods.

The aborigines were sculptors and truffled the mountains
with sensuous bestiaries of coral, obsidian, and jade. They
also hung quantities of seashells from the rafters of their
basket-houses. Once during a violent storm, these shells
created a noise that so enraged Fantasma's ancestor he set the
entire village on fire, thus making room for Pope Publius.
The city's first edifice—a chapel—was built on ground still
warm and strewn with the fatty ashes of burnt bone.

By the time Fogginius arrived, a decade or so later, everything the indigenous population had claimed as "objects of
memory" (or "objects of potency"—the translation is uncertain)—an ancient clump of parrot trees, a crocodile boneyard, a swarm of aerial orchids resembling yellow bees, a
mango grove, and a fairy ring of cultivated gardens—was
gone.

Strangely, the ensuing generations of Fantasmas were
ruled by an obsessive terror that *something should escape
them*—as if that initial conflagration enfevered the brains of
those to follow. This and more: both succeeding generations
had a terror of shells and bones and the sound of hollow
things knocking together, or dangling, or ringing upon the
air. For this reason, the chapel of Pope Publius was the only
one in Christendom never fitted out with a bell. (Because
Old Fantasma had paid for the chapel's construction, the

Designated Powers were willing to overlook this aberration.)

It has been said that Birdland was haunted by the spirits or ghosts of those the Old Fantasma had wronged; that these spirits had escaped through the cyclopean eyes of the basket-dwellings; that these itinerant spirits or ghosts materialized at the foot of a bed, in a chimney or in a high tree, in the privy; rode upon the wind as pollen and seeds, were precipitated during the chiming of a clock, or slept within a bottle of ink, or an imperfectly sealed letter—in other words, manifest so often that if they were not fixed residents, it was common enough to see them or to meet someone who had. So that when they did appear they created no surprise. Only Señor Fantasma went wild when haunted.

And it was said that during the construction of Pope Publius these spirits or ghosts exposed themselves so fearlessly that Señor Fantasma's grandmother was constantly enraged by their incessant interruptions, and driveled on and on to anyone who would listen that, although she would not allow cigars into the house, a uniquely obnoxious phantom insisted on smoking a monstrous black one *in her very own boudoir.* She described him: naked and fiercely hot, his shadowy particulars tattooing the walls as he galloped back and forth upon the bed's counterpane in the moonlight, blowing smoke rings around her nose and causing her lovebirds to throw themselves to their cage's floor in paroxysms of emphysemic terror. To keep the infection from penetrating the hollow recesses of her head, the old biddy went about her business in a veil. For a time it was feared that she had been impregnated by the smoke from the naked ghost's cigar, but chamomile and patience proved the old lady suffered gas.

What is curious is that these were the only spirits to

haunt the island. No one ever saw Señor Fantasma's ancestors sitting in trees or smoking. Fogginius—who eagerly
took down testimony from whomever would give it—and
more testimony from schoolboys than one would think
possible—explained the phenomena thus: heathens cannot
enter heaven and must remain behind to haunt their former
homes, whereas the Old Fantasmas were all Catholics and
had been *seized by heaven whole*. Fogginius feared that if
the Africans—for whom the entire island waited with hope
and misgiving—were not baptized, their spirits, too, would
infiltrate the island—making it inhospitable.

🐚

Such was the world into which little Nuño Alfa y Omega,
called Phosphor, had plummeted. The population of
Birdland was no more than one thousand souls, and it would
have been easy enough to discover the babe's mother and
bring her to reason. But this never occurred to Fogginius.
He believed that, like a worm in cheese, the infant had generated spontaneously upon his door's stoop.

Phosphor's first spoken word was *why*. He had pointed
to the sun and asked his stepfather, *Why?* Until then he had
felt no need to speak, and instead watched with fascination the riot of activity within the scholar's hovel, prodded
through the havoc of pelts, skins, and keeping mediums,
and attempted to make sense out of the weird stories Fa-Fa
told him, those gorgeous lies he believed: that the world was
flat and the excrement of bears so potent one whiff could
kill an elephant.

Damned with crossed eyes, a child who saw everything
in twos unless he squinted, Phosphor was blessed with acute

perceptions. Already at the age of three, when he asked the question *Why*, he had noticed that in finite quantities the atmosphere is transparent—more transparent, even, than water—but that in vast quantities, as in the sky, it was a beautiful blue. Fogginius was aware that the child was no fool, so that when he saw him pointing at the sun and heard the terrible question *Why*, he knew that to answer *Because God* would not give satisfaction. And so he proposed a list, which the longer it grew, the longer it became; a list that, like the snake biting its tail, went on forever:

"Yes!" Fogginius startled the infant by leaping to his feet, "Yes! the *sun! Why?* And why the moon? And why the rain that falls upon our heads? And why do we have heads? And eyes placed at the top of them? Why don't we wear our eyes—as some fishes do—upon our undersides? Why not wear an eye between our buttocks and our anus above our nose? And why, dearest little one—I have often pondered this—do all the animals have faces? Turtles do, and butterflies and ants! Why *life*, Phosphor? And, oh! And, oh! Why, above all, *death?*" Fogginius covered his own face then with his hands, and to the child's dismay began to weep.

Phosphor never forgot the upset his simple question had caused and as he stood blinking and confused, close to tears himself, he vowed he would never ask a question *out loud* again. But it was too late. Wiping his nose with stinking fingers, Fogginius went on:

"Why calamities?" His voice was hoarse. "And evil natures? Black choler, pestilence, and the planets that rotate about the polar star? Why danger and distress? Gall, vinegar, and presages of future things? Alarming flames, little Alfa, omens, anise seeds, imprecations and enchantments? Frogs' mouths? Falling stars? Asparagus? Eclipses? Why do birds have beaks? And if the soul disembarks at death, why must the corporal rind stay behind to corrupt the earth? *And why am I so melancholy?*" Again the scholar sobbed. Phosphor, struck with terror, sobbed too.

Ved—it is now clear to you that Fogginius was a madman determined by magical thinking. His world was fraught with miracles, plagues, and incomprehension. Whereas you and I are the children of Darwin and so have been brought up with the conviction that frogs' mouths and birds' beaks reflect an evolutionary itinerary. And should we discover a dead octopus washed up on the beach and find that it too has a beak (and *very* like a parrot's!) we cannot be too surprised. A familiar melody, The Evolutionary March, swells in our heads; *swells* our heads! Are we not Nature's Crowning Glory? (This—you know me well—I say with a certain bitter irony.)

But back to Phosphor: he is about to come upon the first step in a process that will enable him to capture the world.

2

Fogginius was tyrannical and for the slightest infraction locked his stepson inside his sea trunk, which, as Phosphor grew, seemed to shrink. There, curled in a fetal knot, Phosphor would will himself to sleep, only to awaken screaming, having dreamed of tombs and wells and pits.

One day, as the boy lay helpless and enraged, a beam of sunlight flooded the keyhole. For a few brief moments, Phosphor amused himself by looking at his thumb, first with one eye, then the other. This game caused the thumb to lose its chimerical double and to leap, singly, from left to right. Later he tried this small experiment upon the back of his stepfather's head, and noticed how it too jumped—and how *flat* it looked. One-eyed the boy navigated the room and attempted to dip his pen into the inkpot. Tipping the pot over and onto his knees, he found himself lifted into the air by an ear and once more tossed into the trunk, where he played the same game with the root of his nose. It perplexed him to discover that he seemed to have two noses. Seizing them with his fingers, he was reassured.

Except for the tiny beam of light that collided against the back wall, the trunk was perfectly dark. Having napped

now, rolled into a ball and blinking, Phosphor was startled
to see a projected image of the room's one lopsided window
and of Fogginius suspended before it *upside down*. The effect
was as terrifying as it was magical.

For weeks thereafter, Phosphor taunted his stepfather so
that he would be punished and forced to crouch alone in
the dark. An inventive child, he pocketed a lens from the
scholar's misplaced spectacles and held it to the keyhole. The
image of Fogginius suspended was so sharply reproduced
that, illumined by intuition, Phosphor realized the magician
was not the sordid scholar bent with pitiful patience over a
heap of parrots he had reduced to trash with a savage and
religious passion, *but the sun itself*. The sorcerer was *light*—
not Fogginius, who, if he was capable of talking from dawn
to dusk, could not fry a proper egg.

Fogginius wondered at the eagerness with which his
stepson climbed into the trunk. He supposed that the
boy used its pinching privacy for purposes unclean and so
severely thrashed him. But although he cried out for mercy,
Phosphor forgot his pain because it had come to him that
he must make a miniature model of the trunk in order to
discover the secret laws of holes and beams of light.

"Just as my master thrashes and contains me," the child
reasoned, "and just as the thunder causes it to rain, so it is
possible that light creates images."

The idea that would haunt him for the rest of his days
had begun to take form: that everything visible and palpable
is light; that the world is but a seeming, and, above all, that
form is matter dreaming—an idea he would not articulate for
years but that would, once formulated, inform his creative
life with an exultation born of conviction.

Once when Fogginius had hobbled off in his rags to

hunt the skins of a scarce species of stoat, Phosphor made himself a box, pierced it with a hole, inserted, with some fuss and bother, a tube of black paper, capped it with the lens from Fogginius' spectacles, placed a mirror inside, and lastly, after much tinkering and in an inventive fever, fitted a pane of ground glass onto the top. Light from the little window entered through the lens, was reflected by the mirror onto the glass, which, when manipulated, produced an image of the room in sharp focus. Toying thus, Phosphor stood for hours until, seeing Fogginius' face staring at him from within the box, he was thrust back into the real with a shriek. But instead of thrashing him, Fogginius embraced his stepson.

"You have rediscovered the *camera obscura!*" he cried, and, bursting with pride, congratulated him. Phosphor was disappointed to learn that the black box was not his own invention. But when Fogginius told him that painters used it to trace figures on paper, Phosphor declared:

"A poor use for it! I would *fix* the image and do away with painters!"

"Fix it! Fix it!" The scholar slapped his stepson twice most viciously upon each ear. "I'll fix *you!* Would you thus steal the world from God?" Lifting the box above his head, he sent it crashing into the deeper shadows of the room, exterminating, as he did so, an entire litter of newborn rats.

3

Fogginius was a compulsive describer of climates, and he was also a pamphleteer, his passion for the genre fired by bitterness and the conviction that certain winds are beneficial, moons ominous, the female pudenda perilous. Like the "Clean Sweepers" who would destroy the museum's most precious artifacts because they deem them obscene, Fogginius was bereft of humor.

For a typical day in Pope Publius in the month of July, 1650, Fogginius' journal reads: *Bad air. A break in the moon's halo. By means of which we shall have a wind.*

Trained by a Jesuit theologian also named Fogginius, he once sold his shoes to buy a small red topaz because his master had assured him that, if reduced to powder, the stone would produce a white milk. Fogginius had also proved to his own satisfaction that the moon's influence was moist. Sleeping beneath it upon a high hill, he awoke with a head cold so severe it almost killed him. He had ingested the dung of a sheep for a week because an irresistible voice insisted that the thing must be done else the moon fall into the sea.

"The moon's nature," Fogginius wrote in a pamphlet that

was published in Spain several years before his departure for the island, "is aerial and aquatic." He was successful in his attempt to capture lunar water by leaving little dishes out on the roof on nights when the moon was full. Fogginius sold this dew to a young woman whose underarm hair was so meager it compromised her sexual attractiveness. The hair grew to such profusion that she had not married after all but made her living by sitting on a little gilded chair on market days and raising her arms for the highest bidder. Later she returned to Spain to continue a career which, one hopes, fulfilled her wildest expectations.

A follower of Lactantius, Fogginius ridiculed the theory of the antipodes. He believed the world was flat, a belief that remained unshaken despite his voyage from the Old World to the New. When as a young man Phosphor ran away with merchantmen and was swept by fierce winds to the Polar Circle where he and the entire crew were appalled by an astronomic night six months long, the stepson came to question the stepfather—now so gaga as to suggest to young mothers that they cure their infants' sties by rubbing their eyes with the freshly decapitated bodies of flies.

Entering into maturity, Phosphor refuted Fogginius as "a dangerous fool and a dogmatizer." He had come to question more than his stepfather; he had come to question God. Home again, he could no longer stomach the company of Fogginius. So enraged, so disgusted was he by the codger's lunacies, vanity, and incessant pontifications, and of the thrashings with which he continued to threaten him, that Phosphor became an atheist, shunning all things smacking of mystery, wanting, above all, to profit by the real and so to understand the mechanisms that—as hidden gears animate a music box—cause the world to spin. But, inevitably, such close investigation of the natural world led him back to ineffable mystery. Phosphor then turned to poetry to satisfy a need—the heart's need, perhaps, and the need that mirrored his mind's acute hunger for gnosis.

In the early years of his solitude and independence, Phosphor supported himself by making photogenic drawings of leaves and flowers and the wings of butterflies. These he sold in the market as amulets and, because he was a nonbeliever and a cynic, as "miraculous impressions of the thoughts of angels." Then, by means of a piece of glass painted over with tar and placed in his camera obscura, he was able—centuries before the world at large would learn of such a thing—to capture an instant of time. This first successful experiment plunged him into a chronic fever from which he never entirely recovered.

His next attempt was to create an image *in three dimensions*. Able to focus at close range only, the ocularscope rewarded its inventor with an accurate—if illusory—vision of the three-dimensional world. Because the geometrical axes of the inventor's eyes diverged drastically, the success of the operation was all the more extraordinary. Nuño Alfa y Omega's ocularscope was not only the first stereoscope in Birdland, but the first one in the universe. Thanks to this wonderful machine, a city that exists no more, a world still even to sublimity, is contained as if by magic on flat pieces of glass.

Phosphor's first images were of the natural world. He would capture the exotic fauna of his native island just as Fogginius had done except that in the process nothing would die. Later he captured the sky, the creek-indented beaches, the city of Pope Publius and all its people.

Today as I sit in the National Museum and peer into the ocularscope's twin lenses, the fugitive forms of Phosphor's Birdland appear captured in silver. (Fugitive more than adequately describes this island formed of madrepore, cuttlebone, and sea lime, and which—as you are well aware—ceaselessly changes shape. If it were not for the sea wall circumventing it, pieces of Birdland would be swept away in times of tumultuous weather!)

I have before me the imposing forms of sea turtles sleeping by the hundreds on the beaches; an infant bathing in a barrel; a window brimming with a beauty's yearning face; the mud huts of peons and the empty tombs of voyagers lost at sea; a parrot fish thrashing in a basket; a tortoise fisher; the white moon; a merchant's rug, his cashbox, and his cup; a rhododendron forest; the image of a partial eclipse of the sun as seen imprinted on a garden path through the interstices of the leaves of a lemon tree—a multitude of crescents as numerous as ants; and all the phases of the moon—*phases*, Phosphor might have said, *of the same riddle*.

And now, may I offer you, dear Ved, a *Garden View:*

In the foreground, a fountain—tiered like those banquet trays so favored in the Renaissance, upon which were displayed shellfish or crayfish, or little birds—heads on—or little cakes. The tiers diminish as they rise, and each is brimming with a limpid water. This fountain is surrounded by a circular path which, forking, leads down and away into the very garden where, among pencil-necked cranes, Phosphor will embrace Professor Tardanza's daughter fearlessly, and for the first time.

A Vanitas. Done in the classical manner, it contains a

hollow bone—surely the skull of an aborigine, for it is set out among shells and feather ornaments, and a handful of those ubiquitous glass beads which gave delight before metamorphosing into deadly musket bullets and the teeth of ravenous dogs.

A Ripe Banana Plant. The clustered fruit, bristling and erect, appears to leap out from its sea of leaves, leaves as scored as the ears of bull elephants. There is also a slide of a small plantation of pineapples growing as thickly as thistles in an Irish meadow. Row upon row the fruit rises, an army sabered and plumed.

These pleasure gardens and plantations (and very likely the objects comprising the *vanitas* as well) belonged to Señor Fantasma. His lands were vast, stretching to the sea. They also flanked the city park; later, when Phosphor wanted to take pictures unobserved, he crouched among the pineapples behind an iron fence and spied upon couples strolling the public gardens. A small artificial cascade was visible from within a certain clump of trees, and once Phosphor saw a young woman and her lover take off their shoes and stockings and bathe their feet together in the foam. For a lonely, diminutive man with a clubfoot, the sight was infinitely dolorous. The resulting image is the most poignant of the entire collection.

In those days the women of Birdland wore skirts shaped like bells; the hoops beneath made them appear to levitate. Phosphor was captivated by these ethereal creatures, creatures he believed he could never possess. Yet it seems to me that once one becomes accustomed to the poet's strabismus and the rest, one cannot help but admire the intensity and intelligence of his gaze, his noble features, the beauty of his beard (and his mouth is very fine).

Next: *The Big House*—Old Fantasma's sprawling palace. Twinned spiral staircases, apparently of fossil-studded marble, ascend to the pillared porch. The entrance door, lavishly paned with cut glass, is framed with a garland of aboriginal faces and leaves, and carved of precious wood. To the left one can perceive the hemisphere of the library roof—a library empty of books, but filled with card tables.

The Old Fantasma had a large formal dining room. In it stood a majolica stove and an immense glass-fronted cabinet. This cabinet contained a complete collection of faience dinner dishes entitled *Allegories of the Four Continents*—an encyclopedic series illustrating all the peoples of the world. These figures were portrayed standing in jungly landscapes, their culture's idiosyncrasies largely interpreted by the artist. The younger Fantasma was a man bereft of schooling— although he took great pains to conceal his illiteracy. It was Phosphor's conviction that all Fantasma knew of the greater world he had learned from these dishes and from conversations with Fogginius. Once, in that bleakly sumptuous room, Phosphor, cringing with loathing, listened to Fogginius pontificate upon a dish:

"Just as waterfowl exude a grease to keep them afloat, so the Eskimo exudes a wax that keeps him from desiccating. In his inimitable manner, Yahweh created a distinct species of man exemplarily suited to each part of the terrestrial shelf. The races were meant to be fixed, once and for all, like nails in a door."

❧

My favorite ocularscopic images belong to an evocative series of staged tableaux illustrating apocryphal scenes from vanished indigenous life. The series depicts an aboriginal "queen"—in truth a beauty of the Catalan type—dressed only in her hair and a pair of grass garters. Here she sits in a sled of branches pulled by an armadillo, in a painted landscape opulent with turkeys, toucans, hawksbill turtles, peacocks, parrots, and shells. This beauty suckles a small monkey.

Curiosities of Phosphor's Birdland: sea cows that sailors once took for sirens. An abandoned Dutch settlement at the bottom of a crater. A scarlet shell sporting a white horn—so poisonous one need but see it to die. Mountains truffled with lizards and a sky flooded with birds—many of them mute. (But the lizards continue to whistle, and the beetles to tick like clocks.)

By the way: to my delight, a new exhibit has been installed in what was one of the museum's drearier rooms—a slice of landscape ten feet across and as many deep, and sealed behind glass. It reveals in cross section the lives of those unique clockwork coleoptera from larval stage to burglar nymphs sucking stolen honey, to couples (suspended from string) fertilizing as they copulate those white orchids we once sent, you and I (so long ago!), to Lise Villimpenta—*anonymously*. You are undoubtedly asking at this instant: *Whatever happened to Lise?* She never married, but lives with a black-eyed Cuban named Emelina (which explains, per-haps, a certain mystery we had once attempted to solve). They run a great restaurant on Paradise Street (across from the museum) called the House of the Edible Ark Clam and propose, among other wonders, a palm oil and shrimp dish native to the island, an authentic Cuban *arroz con pollo*, and—hold on to your hat!—*ravioli di zuca al burra versa*! (No danger of meeting up with a "Clean Sweeper" there: the place is far too sensuous!)

4

Ved—the previous descriptions of Phosphor's evocative ocularscopic plates and the revelation of his precipitous invention have me eager to indulge in an "illustrative digression," that is to say, a digression *in your manner:*

As you know, each day aboriginal reliquiae come to light, the most marvelous to date being the cave paintings at Barren Bottoms. I believe there exists a connection between Phosphor's discovery of the capacity of light to steal from reality and produce counterfeits in the form of photographs, and the real seized by the mind of the artist and reproduced by memory upon the walls of a cave—which is another sort of black box. And I wonder: *Is the cave an emblem of the mind? An illustration of how memory functions?* I am suggesting that the painted cave is a representation of the thinking mind, the imagining, the dreaming mind.

Now, all this could be seen as mere idle conjecture except for this: two eyes have been carved above the entrance. And punctuating the vast series of acutely animate creatures are carefully rendered phosphenes of the sort one need only rub one's eyes to see dancing—where? In the mind's eye! Yes—the cave, I am certain, is intended to convey the imagining mind. One enters into it as into a head, a brain, an ideal universe.

In Islam, as you know, to imitate the real is heretical—a mockery of Allah's divine capacities. Was this beautiful place a sacred or a subversive space? (I believe it is sacred and delight in its copulating animals and men. The "Sweepers," appalled by its unabashed ribaldry, are circulating a petition to have the cave filled in.)

❦

I have begun to speak of Señor Fantasma—that nefarious individual is essential to our tale. In the museum's historical wing, a painting dating from the forties and clearly influenced by the surrealists, shows him as the beggar he was to become, and *wearing a tin nose*. His ancestor, the Old Fantasma, stands dressed in Spanish armor before a blazing fire of shells. His skin is pronouncedly blue: as the story goes, he had once thrown himself into a vat of indigo dye—acting out the delirious wish to enter bodily into a process that was making him rich. If it would not have killed him, surely he would have bathed in molten gold. (One of the most unsettling paintings in the entire museum is Bekassim Ortega's *Visitation*—surely you remember it? It shows the aborigines of Birdland standing naked on the beach as inexorably the waves carry the Old Fantasma—standing like a lump of tar in his boat, his features a burning sulphur—to shore. A lethal meteor, he is about to hit the island. The aborigines, seized by an inquisitive stupor, stand feral and untamed—already lost. Their own fires are extinguished and the great pots in which they distill fragrant leaves—their only garment was perfume—are cold, no longer steaming.)

Now back to the grandson: a third portrait—that of the young Fantasma before his ruin—shows a bean pole with flaring nostrils and a beard so black it might have been painted on with ink. It was said that his eyes were sharp enough to bore a hole through a privy wall, or to cause a small dog to wet the ground, yet, paradoxically, his eyes are here unfocused. A despot, Fantasma harbored confusion. Apparently he had no lips; perhaps he has pressed them so tightly shut they have vanished.

Profoundly fearful, Fantasma slept in a marble bed beneath which a stone lion crouched, scowling. (This bed is visible on the museum's second floor landing, as is Fantasma's prie-dieu, washstand, and saddletree. The stone lion, like all the rest, has vanished.)

It is said that from time to time Fantasma's face twisted in a grimace of terror. And that whenever this happened, he looked very like the figure that to this day crouches in the nave of the cathedral grasping both buttocks and revealing the howling face of a sinner about to be voided. (Of the cathedral, little else is worth noting. Nearly four hundred years old, having badly suffered in the earthquake of 1760, it is close to collapse.)

Finally, of Fantasma, a chronicler of the times wrote in the satirical gazette *The Pope's Nose:*

Tymes Fantasma's frighte is suche he trembles on his skinnye legges as doth an ass in fever.

5

Fango Fantasma had one companion: his strongman Yahoo Clay. If Fantasma was cursed with anxiety, Yahoo Clay was damned with rage. He hated a universe that had denied him the capacity to love; for Clay the world was nothing more than the scraphouse of a butchery, a shithouse built upon a graveyard. He said little else than: "Mere buggery."

Pictured in caricature, Yahoo Clay wears an incongruous quantity of hair in the manner of an English judge. According to a chronicler of the time, Clay's acute vanity—which caused him to walk about in clothes queerly fashionable and far too tight—made him appear ludicrous, if, nevertheless, it was evident at a glance that Yahoo Clay was also dangerous.

That Fantasma had hired him was Clay's vindication. Fantasma—in constant fear of assassination, an insomniac who believed in ghosts—felt safer with Clay's bulk beside him. And because women feared him, Clay slept alone, and like a dog, slept on the floor before his master's door.[*]

---

[*] As I am sure you know, Jonathan Swift's dear friend Bishop Berkeley visited Birdland upon his return from Bermuda. It is probable that Swift's Yahoo was, in part, inspired by the tales Berkeley brought home, although Alicia Ombos in

Strangely, Phosphor also slept alone. At a vulnerable age Fogginius had told him an unfortunate story about a maiden whose vulva had been transformed by the machinations of a jealous witch into the jaws of a snapping turtle. From that moment dark places without exits such as ovens and graveyards simultaneously repelled and attracted him. The metaphoric vehicle for his first collection of verse, *The Uncertain Suitor*, is Zeno's paradox. (The poems are so poor I have not included them here.)

Phosphor fell for creatures whose skeletons were as slight as his own—such as Professor Tandanza's daughter, who, to tell the truth, he had seen only once and from a distance; she was sitting on a horse. Because she dreamed of being swept up and away by a centaur (her father was a classicist) and not an impoverished fantast, she ignored Phosphor's epistolary advances, although he made much of the fact that the sound of hooves upon the sod had struck him dumb. He went mad with desire, hallucinating that love had infected him with an incandescent marrow. He sent the girl a poem so peculiar her father instructed the maids not to allow him past the front door under any circumstances:

> *. . . yet I would suck your flesh like milk*
> *else doomed to madness hang*
> *my heart of clay consumed by moss.*

The women who were intrigued by Phosphor's deformities

---

her curious joint critical biography of Nuño Alfa y Omega and Jonathan Swift, *A Swift and a Phosphorous Eye*, claims that, in fact, the name of Fantasma's servant was lost and that popular oral tradition, inspirited by the *Travels*, claimed Yahoo for the tale. This theory is questioned by another scholar, the linguist Heliopolis, who claims the aboriginal word y'ahù (flea-attended; to seethe with rage and loathing; to boil or bubble over) was a common enough colloquialism for thugs on the island already by the early seventeenth century and still popular in the eighteenth. The matter may never be solved.

were megaliths whose ossified husbands reeked of decrepitude, and whose sons had beetled off. These women relished Phosphor's diminutive size—the next best thing to youth—and longed to dandle him on their meaty knees. Sitting on a bench in the botanical gardens, Phosphor would be imagining a virgin so friable one harsh word would suffice to reduce her to powdered sugar, when a creature redolent of moth and rust, and famished for something to brood over, would appear as from a stale crust, and invading the place where he was actively dreaming, press a thigh like a side of butchered beef against his own, letting drop a handkerchief embroidered with an engorged blossom.

It was uncanny how they rooted him out—matrons so amply upholstered that Phosphor fantasized he was about to be crushed beneath an outsize hassock. At moments such as these, Phosphor felt like a gnat in the maw of a frog, like a stone in the gizzard of a hen, like a fly drowning in flan, like a dead rabbit nailed to the side of a barn.

6

One evening Señor Fantasma was walking down Calle Luna y Estrella on his way to the brothel. Nuño Alfa y Omega had a laboratory that opened out onto the street, and that evening he was experimenting with air. He wanted to prove its elasticity. He believed air was "particulated" and that these particles were suspended in quantities and quantities of emptiness. He wanted to prove that the particles could be compressed—he wanted to make compressed air.

Imagine Phosphor in his little laboratory as cluttered as his stepfather's own, blowing air, more and more air, into a globe through a siphon, and then plugging the orifice with his thumb. Just as Señor Fantasma passed by, Phosphor lifted his thumb and the compressed air rushed out of the globe with the sound of thunder. Breaking wind on Mount Olympus, Zeus could not have made a more startling noise.

Nearly knocked off his feet, Señor Fantasma, fearful and curious altogether, peered in at the laboratory's one window and saw all manner of fascinating objects he could not fathom—for example, a thing I have myself examined with perplexity (no small number of artifacts from Phosphor's laboratory may be seen in the municipal museum on

Tuesdays) which may be the universe's first periscope—
retorts, distorting mirrors, a reflecting microscope, various
meteorological instruments, a rudimentary phosphoro-
scope, two conquistadors' metal helmets soldered together
in such a way as to form a species of pressure-cooker, the
inventor's laundry and stew pot—the whole illuminated by
two filthy oil lamps.

Because of the semidarkness and the noise, and the
unrecognizable smells—for Phosphor was also experimenting with various collodion techniques—Señor Fantasma
thought he had stumbled upon the laboratory of a puissant
magician. He had heard that magicians spoke to demons
by means of brass pipes or tubes of glass, and a great many
of those were lying about.

Fantasma was fascinated by the experiment with the glass
globe and asked Phosphor to repeat it several times. He was
curious about everything he saw—the bottles of Etruscan
wax and fossil salts, the laxatives and bitumous trefoil, the
stone magnets, and, above all, a rudimentary camera that
perplexed him utterly—and frightened him too, so that he
did not dare ask its purpose.

Soon his gaze fell upon a large blue bottle filled to the
brim with a granulous black gum. The gum was a concoc-
tion of burned bees boiled in olive oil and Athenian honey
sixty-six times. The stuff had been made to be worn on the
head as a poultice and was proven, already by the Greeks,
to prevent loss of hair. In fact the stuff in the bottle had
been prepared by Fogginius, and when Phosphor had abandoned his stepfather, he took it with him as a reminder of
the old man's foolishness. But he did not tell this to Señor
Fantasma, who, he could see—by the quantity of silver he

wore, his lace cuffs, and perfumed beard—was both very rich and a man whose brow was precipitously receding.

Phosphor was living in acute poverty, and when his visitor asked the bottle's price, he sold it to him. As Señor Fantasma left the laboratory with the bottle clutched to his ribs, the street resounded once again to the cosmical retort.

The second time Fantasma visited Phosphor's laboratory, a thick tuft of red hair—much like a cock's comb—had taken root in his scalp. Convinced now of Phosphor's fantastical powers, Fantasma asked to see what other marvels he had to offer up for sale. Phosphor unwrapped those magicked images he had freshly seized with his black box and showed his visitor a small portrait of his landlady, Señora Portaequipajes, wearing a white lace collar and produced on photo-sensitized silver-plated copper—"a procedure," Phosphor did not fail to impress upon Fantasma, "ruinously expensive."

Frankly astonished, Fantasma turned the little boxed image this way and that before the laboratory's one window. He had never seen such a thing before. No one had.

As within the magic mirror of a necromancer—which is exactly what Fantasma believed he held in his hand—Señora Portaequipajes' bristling face broke forth only to vanish, breathed and then expired, flared up and faded out, materialized and went up in smoke. Señor Fantasma held his breath. A monkey with a looking glass could not have been more startled. "It is," he said, amazed, "*alive!*" And he brayed with cruel laughter. Ever after, Fantasma would think of Phosphor's ability to produce images as miraculous.

"Have you others?" Phosphor handed him another. This time Señora Portaequipajes' mouth was open as if she would speak. Phosphor had kept her sitting far too long, and she had lost patience. Her sharp teeth flashed and leapt from the enchanted surface like tiny candle flames.

As Fantasma looked with admiration upon Señora Portaequipajes' unpleasant face, Phosphor explained that he wished to produce a set of scientific portraits illustrating the multiple aspects of human emotion: grief, terror, delight, envy, ecstasy, and so on. One supposes that Fantasma, a cold and indifferent man, at once realized he might hugely benefit from Phosphor's project, because he proposed to finance it. Thus, thanks to the inventor's multitudinous study, Fantasma learned to read the faces of his fellow men as in a book: line by line. (And to reflect with his own those emotions he did not feel.)

Fantasma gave Phosphor more money than he had ever seen to buy the copper, silver, glass, and other things he needed, including the equipment to build a portable black box containing a separate dark chamber wherein the negative process, from start to finish, could be performed anywhere. Phosphor threw himself into this work, and soon the walls of his little laboratory were orbited by faces collapsed in terror, condensed in pain, distorted by anxiety, centrifugal with desire.

At first Phosphor continued to use Señora Portaequipajes as a model, but her face was really too fat and she too agitated; she suffered from a chronic inflammation of the gums and other disorders. (Like Phosphor, she had a lazy eye that had a tendency to lodge itself with fixity to the left of the bridge of her large nose.) Phosphor looked for models elsewhere. A mere infant at the time, howling for his supper, Señora Portaequipajes' own son is stuck forever behind glass.

Next Phosphor hired Rosendo Cosme—a once-famous actor with a face of rubber who, down and out, sat for the black box with renewed pride. As it turned out, Cosme had a fourteen-year-old daughter, Cosima, whose beautiful face was mobile, too. Cosima posed pouting, smiling, weeping, languishing; there are portraits of her determined, unsure, indignant; portraits of Cosima clenching her pretty teeth, uncovering one canine in a sneer; her eyes hooked to heaven in prayer; Cosima shrinking in disgust; Cosima eating a mango, a green lemon; smoking a cigar.

Señor Fantasma was delighted with the pictures and more: he desired the infant actress from the instant he saw the perfect planet of her little face screwed up in mock despair. More than once, while her father sat counting coins in his filthy kitchen, Señor Fantasma had his way with her.

"God has secret cabinets of the precious things he keeps far from the eyes of men," Señor Fantasma said to Phosphor. He was thinking of those fabulous mines his grandfather, the Old Fantasma, had sucked dry. "And so shall I have a secret cabinet of images unlike any in the world. You will come with me the next time I visit Cosima in her hovel."

For the sake of Art and Science (and, frankly, because he was disgusted with poverty) Phosphor went. Included in the arrangement was all the material he needed to continue and more—for he was conducting experiments in the attempt to photo-sensitize other surfaces—such as zinc. Already he was dreaming of the ocularscope, and even in his dreams continued on his quest to discover the secrets of bifocal vision.

Ved—I wish to add here that an entirely new room has been

opened in the museum, an oval and ethereal room painted blue and filled with the skeletons of simple marine animals: Neptune's chariots and other treelike corals, and the crazed meandrina—so like a maze, so like a human brain.

Wonderful as these treasures are, they are outdone by a stunning reproduction of the island of Birdland itself—which is nothing more than a great egg made of the multitudinous skeletons of creatures acutely fragile and transient.

Like many coral islands, Birdland is oval, shaped like the world or the orbit the world makes about the sun. It is a curious thing that an island formed of creatures the size of a pin should be surrounded by water so deep that beyond the shallow bays—themselves coral shelves protected by coral reefs—the bottom has never been measured.

It is impossible to describe the beauty of this plaster model of my island. It includes a variable green ocean painted in transparencies so that the rendering of the depths and shallows is hallucinatory. The ocean appears to swell, to embrace the island with an eager affection. Clearly the artist has what you, dear Ved, call a "sexual soul."

The painted sea is cunningly laced with foam that, at Sand Point and Half Moon Reef, bristles into furious breakers; minute fishing boats are poised here and there on invisible pins and the artist has lovingly placed wee coconut palms the size of needles on the coral reefs. In fact, the island's lush vegetation has been duplicated so cleverly that for several instants altogether it is possible to imagine one is silently navigating the air above Birdland in a balloon.

I cannot express how delightful it is within the oval room to contemplate the bodies of the astraeans, the millepora, corallines, madrepores, and meandrina that have, over millennia, caused the island to be, and simultaneously contemplate the island itself, as if *magicked* into miniature and pulsing with life.

Hanging near the exit, an astonishing series of pencil drawings describe the entire life cycle of the coral—from the birth of the egg-shaped larva to the first form of the polypidom. Most discreetly, in the lower lefthand corner, each is signed: Polly. (By the way, an aquarium completes this room, in which living, plumy corals, millepores, algae, and vibrantly crowned sea anemones, adhering to the glass, attract the visitor's attention by waving their arms.)

Today the island was rocked by an unusually violent storm; the pebble cobbles of the streets all blackened beneath a hazy, fragrant rain. Sipping wine on Paradise Street I wondered: *Who is this Polly?* Has she arrived from elsewhere? Rushing out into the thundering afternoon, I returned to the museum to ask the custodian—Old Moss Mouth— about her. I was told that, a native of the island, she has recently returned from New Zealand—the new curator of the natural history collections.

She's awfully good, Ved. I contemplated her mock-up of the island for a full two hours altogether—with a species of elation!

7

The first three-dimensional image Phosphor produced was of Cosima sitting navel-deep in a tub of water. Around her slender neck she wears a silver cross—a gift from Señor Fantasma—and the tub, as well as her knees and elbows (as are her shoulder blades) are all revealed in luminous and dramatic relief. Her great head of hair appears to be burning.

What is curious about this picture, extraordinary in fact, is Cosima's face. She is gazing at the photographer with an expression I can only describe as a cross between ferocious complicity and defiance. Cosima's eyes appear to be saying: *Yes. I am his hireling for now! But the slave shall outsmart the master: wait and see!*

Until then, Cosima had seen herself in her father's mirror: a large oval of polished steel, it had offered her an infinite stage and an interminable sequence of dramatic situations. A passionate dreamer, a little tigress, she dreamed of pirates, of performing in scarlet skirts on a sailing ship the size of a small country, dreamed of dancing under a rain of gold and silver money. The mirror delivered to Cosima her essence— that of a creature of the instant who appeared to be there but who was always elsewhere. Whatever Cosima did, she did because her mirror had told her that she looked beautiful doing it. The mirror taught her to weep with an unfurrowed brow, to laugh in such a way that her brown throat, softly pulsing, was heartbreakingly visible.

Like Petronius' silver doll, she was a gorgeous automaton—and this should come as no surprise: when Cosima was but an infant, her father had, with the help of a switch, harsh words, and harsher threats, with stays and pins and a clever use of rouge, transformed his daughter into a mechanical toy. Each Saturday Cosima performed in the marketplace from dawn to dusk until she dropped.

And the mirror gave Cosima the power not only to leave the confines of her room and body, but to double those few meager treasures she had found in the street after a performance when, for example, she had played the monkey to her father's organ. These she kept hidden from Cosme's avaricious eye: a large pearl earring, a bent silver cat's-eye brooch, and one brass ring.

Phosphor hated the way Fantasma had reduced Cosima— far more than fate had done. He gave her an image of herself that she could carry everywhere. Whenever Cosme's threats and Fantasma's fucking threatened to submerge her in wretchedness, she took hold of the image of a blossoming child contained within its little hinged box—so like a reliquary—and felt powerful again, fearless too; somehow secure. This image was more than a mirror: it was the hearth by which she warmed herself, a miniature altar at which she could worship her own inviolable soul. For, if badly bruised, Cosima was not broken. Her capacity to *seem* rather than *be* had protected her.

Cosima's eyes were so like her own mother's eyes—eyes

that had once gazed upon her with delight—that the certitude she had once been loved, and deeply, was hers each time she opened the little box. And no matter how miserable she was, how tattered, the image always showed a girl combed and scrubbed, and wearing a precious lace mantilla, draped and pinned in such a way one could not see it was full of holes.

Cosima's face is illumined by the moon of a solitary pearl—although, gazing at it now, I could say it is the pearl that is illumined by the moon of Cosima's beautiful face. (Yes! The image exists: catalog #444.) Clearly the photographer had not stolen his subject's soul, but instead, secured it—a tangible kernel of shadow and light.

Interestingly, Phosphor never thought of his invention as more than a toy. "My black box seizes reality," he wrote somewhere, "it does not *reveal* anything." It seemed to him that words evoked more than images. "In the beginning was the *word*," he later would joke with Tardanza. "We are still waiting for the *light*." Knowing this about him, we may now move on to the next chapter.

8

Señor Fantasma had been suffering from various and often contradictory ailments: pains in the head and soles of the feet, somnolence and photophobia, nightmares in which his body was so riddled with arrows that he could hear the wind whistle through all his parts.

Fogginius, who had long been his private surgeon, poked and prodded him rigorously; told him he suffered Hot Lungs, Dry Liver, Constricted Heart, and Cold Brain. He prescribed the stale urine of geese, head baths, fresh air and exercise, and suggested Fantasma occupy his addled and gloomy mind with novelty—else succumb to irreversible debilitation.

Simultaneously, Phosphor was slapped on the head with the conviction that, if he was to survive fatality, he must put his native island to paper, write a piece of epic poetry in which Birdland would be a metaphor for something—he knew not yet what.

So moved was he by the clarity with which his destiny had revealed itself, that at the table of the inn in which he celebrated his change of fortune, he set to at once and within the hour produced a prodigal set of verses—purged,

he believed, of frivolity and excess—and which described
the savor of a dish of snails stewed in oil and garlic and
nine grains of pepper; described the jovial innkeeper and
the diabolically beautiful face and body of his youngest
daughter who was preoccupied with the plucking of a hen;
observed and noted the evening's astrological conditions;
discussed several incidents of local interest involving fraud-
ulent females; and lastly: how once as an infant wading in
the sea he had been badly pinched by a giant crab of the
Anomoura family.

Concurrently, just as Phosphor succumbed to sleep,
digesting snails and dreaming of immortality, Fantasma's
strongman Yahoo Clay committed a crime. He was caught
and ordered to leave the city for a full six months, else, in
the language of the law: *hang 'til his bowels emptie into his
shoes.*

Perspiring within his yellow wig, Clay took himself to
his master's door. There, among the lizards, he waited for
dawn when he would inform Fantasma that their plot to
smoke a rival like a leg of pig had backfired when, delivered
to the butcher's in a sack, the victim, despite his bruises, had
resurrected and screamed.

As Clay caught beetles and toyed with a lizard, blinding
it with thorns to pass the time, and as Phosphor slept,
Fantasma dreamed of the ocularscope. He saw himself sitting alone beneath a candelabra brightly lit, leisurely turning
a crank—which was, somehow, also his own erect member—as Birdland unfolded before him. He awoke exultant:
had he pictures enough, he could seize the entire island.
He would hire Nuño Alfa y Omega to produce an interminable set of three-dimensional images, and he would fur-
nish everything necessary toward the construction of an

ocularscopic box large enough to contain one thousand plates. (Because Fantasma had not learned to count, one thousand signified an infinite quantity.)

And so, in one night, all things came together to make the mold that was to shape these lives. Shortly after dawn, Señor Fantasma, having paid off the authorities and calmed Clay's fears, set off for the minuscule house Phosphor rented from Señora Portaequipajes. Once there he beat upon the door with his fists. Phosphor's servant Pulco went careening to see who the visitors might be. Throwing the door aside, Pulco saw the thug and his master standing rigid with purpose in the haze.

Little Pulco had heard of Clay's crime—everybody had— and he was terribly frightened. Clay, who was constantly on the lookout for children to bribe, pulled out a bag of sweets from his purse and, bending down, poked one into the boy's mouth.

"Where is your master?" he asked, nearly cramming the candy down Pulco's throat. Too frightened to speak, Pulco leapt over the threshold and ran to the inn where he roused Phosphor by pounding his hump. Home again, they found Yahoo Clay peering down the necks of bottles looking for wine. And although Phosphor was concerned lest the brute break something irreplaceable, his thoughts were at once taken over by Fantasma's urgent proposal.

At first Phosphor believed Fantasma was planning an insurrection. Several minutes passed before he realized what Fantasma's urgent babbling was all about.

"We will embrace the island," he ranted, "coast to coast. We will take maidens, the eyes of volcanoes, the shadows of pontiffs, clothes on the line, the bitter and the sweet, the features of natural scenery, all articles of luxury, ducking stools and stirrups and the seasons, too! We will eat the memories of others, freeze time, rape space and in three dimensions, too! None of your *flat* pictures, Omega! But the ones with elbow room! *The entire island, see?* We will forget nothing!" Fantasma was nearly dancing, a thing strange to behold.

"I shall have it all," he cried, "captured in silver," he salivated, "on glass." Knots appeared in his neck as if invisible fingers were playing upon the tendons.

As Fantasma spoke, Clay continued to poke among the inventor's things. When he knocked over a set of scales and weights, Phosphor nearly jumped from his skin. He was not much used to company.

Señor Fantasma was proposing an extravagant salary. Never again would Phosphor live in poverty. From that day on he would dine on suckling pig. Phosphor must begin packing at once; he and Pulco would move into a wing of the Big House and there prepare for the journey.

The arrangement could not be refused, yet it made Phosphor nervous. From now on he would be Fantasma's puppet, producing images to satisfy Fantasma's greed.

Fantasma took Pulco on his knees. "Imagine," he said as he nibbled the tender lobe of the boy's ear, frightening him—and with good reason—"you'll sleep in a bed and eat flan off precious china like a princess! You'll roam gardens at your leisure and piss in the roses like the lapdog of a queen!"

Pulco did not know if he should laugh at this news or weep. Although Clay had stuffed his cheeks to the point of bursting, Fantasma managed to squirrel another sugarplum between his lips.

It was at this moment that Clay believed he had found

what he was after. Uncorking a bottle with his teeth, he sniffed and guzzled down a half-liter of an elixir Fogginius had once hoped would render him immortal or, at the very least, invisible, and that Phosphor now sold by the spoonful to housewives in need of roach poison.

The fracas the thug made was terrible. As the others watched (save for Pulco who had seized the occasion to vomit candy onto the street) Yahoo Clay metamorphosed into a grunting bear, a raging dragon, a defecating pig. He changed color, appeared to swell, to shrink, to swell again. He threw himself upon Phosphor's laboratory table as if into a pool of deep water, spitting bile and a green wine reeking of goat shit, violets, and acetic acid.

❧

Dear friend, I shall now engage in a brief digression precipitated by your recent letter, in which you ask about Alicia Ombos' study *A Swift and a Phosphorous Eye*. Her theories are strange and compelling; for example, she finds the key to Swift's vision in the great voyages of discovery of the previous centuries, which, she claims, *revealed a sprawling world infinitely stranger than previously imagined*. A world of wonders, then, and this reflected in the *Wunderkammern* or cabinets of marvels in which the world's sprawl could be comfortably contained as though so much savage and eccentric beauty—fulgent birds with beaks the size of luggage, pigs castellated with tortoiseshell, snakes as broad as chimneys—could be assimilated in homeopathic doses only. She writes:

The fantastic influx of curiosities precipitated by engagements in new worlds had a profoundly unsettling effect upon

pedestrian and pious minds convinced the finite world was cre-
ated reasonably, to the measure of man, and for man's salvation.
She goes on to demonstrate that if the marvelous incites
wonder, it also evokes fear. Those nest-building men of the
woods so like human parodies with their *incontournable*
noses, scatological habits, and blatant sexual lives must have
badly cracked the egos of men and women who flattered
themselves made in God's image. If men and women looked
like God and *Semnopithecus nasica* like clownish man, then
God had a little of the monkey, too, and the universe illumined more brightly by monkeyshine, perhaps, than by the
flames of votive candles. Darwin, dear Ved, is just a sneeze
away!

The insult culminates in Jonathan Swift's Yahoo—that
cursed, hairy animal that cures its own evil by eating its own
excreta—a practice popular in both Swift's and Phosphor's
day and, as insalubrious as it was, still safer than the cos-
metic use of white lead (see Swift's "Progress of Beauty").

Because it sufficed that a thing be rare or strange to find
its way into a *Wunderkammern*, the collections were as inco-
herent as they were astonishing, imposing a new genus:
extraordinem. A species of distillation, the cabinets reveal
an existential stance; Ombos argues: *an attempt to seize and*
fix a universe in constant flux. Their purpose is born as much
from terror as delight. And if the Divine Architect had created an alphabet too vast to decipher even after a lifetime
of intense scrutiny fortified by faith, the cabinet afford a
raccorci, a reassuring microcosm, prefigured in (and perhaps
inspirited by) Columbus' *ambulant cabinet*, his encyclopedic
entry into Barcelona, which included live parrots, precious
plants, and painted Indians further objectified by the gold
ornaments they wore.

Within the wonder rooms, the natural world is ordered in ideal display; ideal because confined to a closet—unassociated, disaffiliated, isolated, and irrelevant—the elements that once made up a living tissue can only be dreamed. As beautiful as these collections are, they betray a rupture at the heart of things and reveal a world that has never ceased to fester, a chronic blindness also, an incapacity to read—not only the world's body but its metaphysical books of days and dreams and prophesies. (And I am thinking of the painted books of the Mexica reduced to ashes.) It is as though God gave man a second chance at Eden, and man, that confirmed shopkeeper, could not dwell there but only sell there.

9

Yahoo Clay's banishment was postponed until the instant he would be fit to travel—although it would not be certain for some weeks that he would even survive. He was tended by Fantasma's personal doctor, who was, as you know, no other than Phosphor's hated stepfather, Fogginius.

Now so old as to be bent in two and nearly blind, Fogginius used his nose both for navigation and as a probe, rudely prodding people in the buttocks and at table ruining the perfect geometry of a rice pilaf or a gelatin pudding. When he peered into his stepson's face for the first time in two decades, he thought he saw the cook and asked at once for milk soup. Informed of his mistake, and introduced to Nuño the inventor, Fogginius, his nose poking Phosphor's navel, apologized to Nulo the impersonator.

Fogginius tended to Clay with a soup of slimes boiled twelve times in honey; with tincture of marshmallow and fumigations of texts written on veritable Egyptian papyrus in invisible ink; he blew air into Clay's festering lungs through the windpipe of a whooping crane.

These were the sanest elements of the cure; Clay was also given a purse of wet sheep dung to wear on his stomach, and as he could barely move—so labored his breathing (and the man wept each time he had to swallow)—he complied with Fogginius' demands and lay immobile and wheezing, the purse of dung burning like an infernal castigation.

Meanwhile, Señor Fantasma prepared for the necromantic voyage by ordering all the equipment required and outfitting the mules to Fogginius' specifications. He had the cook prepare a compact and inedible bread made of popcorn and mud.

Phosphor concerned himself with the task of producing travelers' spectacles for everyone, including his stepfather, who—as he could not tell the difference between a bird cage and a breadbox—was about to be totally incapacitated. Although they would spend many months together side by side, Fogginius would never recognize the stepson he had once so liberally thrashed.

Phosphor also saw to it that each traveler owned a sunshade for those instances when they would be continuing along the exposed coast or across the island's notorious badlands. He also provided sandals, for many points of interest could not be reached by mule. (The paved and cobbled roads that now net the island, to the felicity of the curious tourist, date from the early part of the twentieth century.) Little Pulco proved to be a serious apprentice cobbler, and the task of sandal-making was left to him.

❧

Because Clay's recovery was tedious and protracted, Phosphor and little Pulco had plenty of time to accommodate themselves to their new environment. Pulco slept in the kitchen on a little pallet of fresh straw; for the first time in his life, Phosphor slept in a bed between clean sheets. They took their breakfast—of eggs and fruit and sugared rolls and fresh coffee and jams: of rose petals, of quinces, of peaches, of limes—in the great kitchen, which opened out on a sunny veranda smelling of freshly washed shirts and the hot bodies of roosting hens. However, despite the luxury of their surroundings, Clay's battle with death permeated the entire house. Even the weather appeared to be affected.

During all the weeks of Clay's convalescence, the sky was like lead. Once after urinating, Fogginius declared he had produced lava. Gazing in a mirror, little Pulco was surprised to see his face had not melted in the heat. The cook declared she felt as heavy as a plum boiled twelve times in sugar. Even when freshly bathed, they all attracted flies.

"We are creatures of lead," Fogginius repeated more often than necessary, "and drunk on it." And he held with both hands the hard, hollow bone that barely contained his reeling thoughts, and shuddered.

A few weeks after his mishap, Clay's fever worsened. His breathing was so bad one could hear his lungs rattle throughout the Big House. That evening the cook dug up a mandrake in the kitchen garden. Headless, sexed like a man, it had two strange little arms and hairy legs. Although it squirmed in her hand, she brought it into the kitchen and with a sharp knife she severed the mandrake from its leaves. Although it continued to kick, she washed it well in water and vinegar and put it in a deep bottle with plenty of good pear brandy. For an hour it floated at the top, but then it dropped and hung thereafter suspended in the middle, immobile and silent. (When the museum put up various miscellanea for auction last spring, I was tempted to purchase it, but didn't.)

For weeks, only the mandrake and the moon floated; everything else was weighted down. Phosphor's clubfoot pained him and he began to look upon the imminent voyage with trepidation. However, Clay, taking bouillon daily and even a poached egg, was still too ill to travel.

. One afternoon, as little Pulco sat in the kitchen poking holes into leather, a dragonfly sailed in through the open door to lay her eggs in a dish of water. She was immense, gorgeous, green and yellow to the tip of her tail, which was a metallic blue. This tail was pronged, a claw or hook, and so bowed in sexual tension that Pulco feared it would snap in two. As her eggs tumbled into the dish, Pulco clasped his hands and his heart hammered.

Sometimes in the early evening, as Phosphor ground the lenses of the travelers' spectacles (and he had already perfected a folding tripod that could be screwed to the base of his black box), Pulco sat in the garden shed. It smelled of baking, of the wings and bodies of all the things which, trapped there, were gradually reduced to dust.

In the shed, Pulco played with the tubers and bulbs—many imported from Holland or Brazil, or even the Orient in pine crates stuffed with straw. Or he wandered Fantasma's overgrown gardens, which were always empty. Sometimes he sat among the ripening pineapples and listened to the gardener pumping water from the deepest well—the only well not dry—to soak the roots of the alligator pears, the mangos, zopotillas, and the blazing pepper plants. The sand paths, stiff with salt, glistened.

When the paths were damp from waterings, and as the water evaporated, butterflies settled. In those days in Birdland, there were so many butterflies entire trees were often hidden by their tremulous wings. The coastal hills blazed scarlet, bronze, or blue during their seasons of copulation.

Once, still as a stone, Pulco watched as an Adonis sat in the path and collected the cool air under its wings. When the Adonis settles, it closes its wings and vanishes. Only when it flies, zigzagging in the air, do its bright violet wings catch the eye. In this way it is very like Pulco; crouching in the shadows he melts away, but when he moves he is highly visible. Lurching first this way, then that, he too zigs and zags.

Often in the late morning when Pulco had completed his tasks, he explored the Big House, its tiled corridors with windows opening onto fragrant, if seedy, courtyards. Or he played in the kitchen with toys once belonging to the cook's daughter, little Tina, who died extravagantly as she played Hide and Seek among the bananas—beheaded, accidentally, by a harvester's machete. The games Pulco played were circumscribed by his own imperfect infancy: he imagined things too precisely, he felt things too acutely, and his mind had a tendency to move in ruts. If the game veered into the unexpected, or took up a dark course, Pulco became frightened and sometimes he shrieked.

It was Pulco's conviction that the world was ruled by Six Persons who had once climbed out of a hole. In his games he found this hole, more nidus than abyss, and the Six rewarded him with freedom from tasks and a family. Pulco described the Six so precisely that the cook, overhearing his childish prattle, would see them too—huddled together in the deep shadows, forming a sinister circle—Africans and Eskimos and Indians—like the ones on Señor Fantasma's faience dishes. She can see the Choctaw warrior dressed in nothing but a garland of clotted scalps, the Chinaman just as Marco Polo described him—sword in hand—and suddenly little Pulco is shrieking, his shrieks tear the air like a flock of startled crows.

Whenever little Pulco begins to shriek, the cook sinks to her knees and holds him until, feeling better, he can tell her another secret dream: one day to make for his master, Nuño Alfa y Omega, *a shoe with wheels.*

Pulco draws a picture so that the cook can see just how these shoes should be. He next draws his master's feet—one perfect, the other shaped like a hammer. Pulco explains that it cannot be cut off; it is as much a part of his master as the eyes burning in his skull, his beating heart, his thinking brain:

Near the end of August, Yahoo Clay rose from his bed. It was Phosphor's conviction that it was not, as Fogginius insisted, the action of the waning moon, nor the dung upon his heart, nor the soup of slimes he had ingested every day for sixty days, but rather that Clay could no longer stomach Fogginius.

As he had tottered above the pit of death, Clay had endured the circuitous legend of Saint Sousmyos, had, against his will, considered the progressive and retrograde motions of the stars, the nature of the souls of animals, the divinity of the number six. He had heard named and counted all the bones of the body. He had considered the fact—gruesome to Fogginius—that all the magical paraphernalia of Simon Magus lies rotting at the bottom of the sea; Fogginius could not recall which sea. When one late afternoon Fogginius proposed readings from the Latin glossary of Ansileubus "to entertain and occupy his patient's mind," Clay, bleating the sound a sheep makes just as its throat is slit, heaved himself up and away. Thereafter, he could not speak—for weeks, that is—but only bleat. This did not interfere with his function; Señor Fantasma needed the thug for a shield from dangers less real than imaginary. Shield and shadow, Clay's voice had always been superfluous.

❧

Ved—the compilation of all this material has, thus far, taken up the better part of the winter. Profoundly, inconsolably alone, a man without a love (and so, as you once said, *without a home*), I decided to re-create a world that is—save for threads and tatters, "feathers and fables"—forever lost. My passion for the island's early history decided me to devote myself to one extraordinary moment (and person: Nuño Alfa y Omega)—and this, dear Ved, for you.

If at the outset I was, in particular, intrigued by Phosphor's extreme precocity and the beauty of his images on metal and glass, the plight of four lonely men (and one innocent child) on a pilgrimage of sorts could not help but fire my imagination. Sometime during the winter—that glorious season of intense verdure and daily rains—it came to me that *love offers the only intimation of eternity.* That it is the loveless men, those incapable of profoundly feeling, who scrabble after fame and power. Because their life is, in fact, the other face of death.

These reflections bring me back to Swift's curiously loveless life; after all, he kept his Stella in a box as though she too were far too *curious* or monstrous to be "let loose"! I have been rereading what Alicia Ombos calls his spy-glass poems: those poems in which the suitor explores his absent lady's chambers, putting his nose into the very things that cause his virility to recoil in horror. It is clear that for Swift, *femaleness* is the lie that conceals the bitter bones of truth. He cannot forgive the flesh because it dies; he cannot forgive woman the transitory physicality that defines, determines (and damns) him, too. In these poems, the distinctions between the real and the false, corruption and health, sex and death are abandoned and the rifts between them, in Ombos's words, *lizard in all directions until the landscapes of these burgled rooms swell and crack as though in the throes of intense seismic upheaval.*

Returning at midnight, Ombos continues, *that exemplary hour of revelation, Corinna pulls off her hair and plucks out her eye. Her macabre striptease reveals that she is nothing more than a species of upholstered coffin: tacks, tassels, and padding removed, all that remains is an eager abyss* (eager because once abed the hag lies tormented by dreams of love!).

For Swift, Time is female and it is female flesh that, above all things, epitomizes Swift's own terror of dissolution. Perhaps the cyclical cacophony that tortured him throughout his life (he was a victim of Ménière's disease) translated into an acute perception of the particulating world. Was Swift's wounded inner ear particularly sensitive to the sound of Her minuscule but incessant teeth? In any case, the passage of Time, above all in Swift's poems, is accelerated to a vertiginous degree; like particles in an atomic cannon, matter fractures and dissolves before our eyes:

> *. . . And this is fair Diana's Case;*
> *For, all Astrologers maintain*
> *Each Night a Bit drops off her Face,*
> *while Mortals say she's in her Wain.*
> —"The Progress of Beauty"

Writes Ombos: *I would suggest that Swift distrusts both voids—fore and aft (mouth and anus)—as acutely as he distrusts the "visions" (or "humors," or the guts) in between; that his imagination pierces to deflate; that the eye of Swift's needle is as sharp as its tip; that the vision is a species of sprawling body that will not be contained: the body as landscape, quicksand, as bog; the world an ogress riddled with orifices, littered with dung (in which Gulliver/Swift so often finds himself "in the middle up to my knees").*

But I fear these reflections have little place here in this history that reads more like a fable! I can hear your stern criticism: *Don't burden your book with IDEAS!!!*

Back to the tale. . . .

10

Unaware that the moon had waned to a cuticle, Fogginius insisted Clay walk every evening for one hour beneath its beneficial radiance. One night, as Clay wheezed among the coconuts, Phosphor, Fogginius, and Fantasma sat together in heated discussion on the balcony: How would the completed ocularscopic *theatrum mundi* be classified within its viewing box? For example, should women be viewed with mammals of all sorts, or confined to districts, or according to age or beauty? Could the image of Señora Portaequipajes stooped scowling over a slop pail be viewed an instant after the beautiful Cosima in her bath? What were the philosophical, the cosmical implications of such a juxtaposition? And what of statuary? And did the eggs of hens belong with eggcups or with barnyard scenes (including cows) or in a gastronomical series? Were musical instruments a species of furniture? Phosphor was no longer listening. Instead, he wondered: Could *sound* also be seized on glass?

At that moment, Cosme appeared in a cinnamon tree high above them. Leaping to the balcony and executing a mock salute, he informed Señor Fantasma that Cosima was big with child. Fantasma paled, reddened, paled again, and thinking to buy him, tossed Cosme a purse, which the actor caught in his teeth with prodigious alacrity.

Then, stuffing it down a codpiece bursting with pilfered eggs—hard-boiled—and grinning ear to ear, Cosme announced that the priest would arrive instantaneously.

Fantasma declared the thing impossible—he could not, he *refused* to marry an infant. And reaching for a blacking brush that earlier had served Fogginius in a lengthy demonstration upon the nature and function of levers, he bounded to his feet and made to crack open the actor's skull.

All this time Cosima had been hiding behind the balcony door. She now appeared holding a belly as round as a terrestrial globe. Indeed, had Professor Tardanza been there, he would surely have recognized the form of an object that had vanished from his rooms but a week before, along with a pair of newly varnished boots.

Illumined by a lantern, Cosima stood defiantly before them, her eyes both wet with tears and very black. Standing there in her frail bones and ruddy cheeks, she looked so lovely that had Fantasma a heart in his breast and not a desiccated turd, it would have melted. Yet, because the babe was clearly incubating, its mother's eyes flashing, its grandfather executing cartwheels on the balustrades, and the priest, his mouth sweetened with kitchen crumbs, now floating across the floor in their direction—the thing was done. And so swiftly that Fantasma was forever convinced he had been screwed by sorcerers and charlatans—which, undoubtedly, was true.

Later Cosima was given a bath by the cook and taken to her master's bed. Shortly thereafter, Fantasma was heard to cry out—in pain or pleasure, no one could say. He wandered down to breakfast, his pride badly shaken; apparently the night before, when he had reached for Cosima's breasts, she had bitten his hand.

When Fogginius, plagued by perpetual fog, stumbled into the kitchen wanting butter (for a blister occasioned by the harness he wore to keep his intestines from dropping out of his anus) and collided with the ripe melon of Cosima's fictive belly, he insisted she follow a cure for rotundular air.

Bewildered, Cosima looked on as Fogginius took up a mortar and pestle and proceeded to manufacture pills. It is fortunate that the sage did not harm her: Cosima thrived upon the ashes of asps, calf fat, and beeswax.

❧

In the early part of the day, as the kitchen filled with light and the smells of baking, Cosima combed out Pulco's matted hair and told him stories. She inquired after Pulco's parents, but Pulco was a thing of spontaneous generation: he had materialized on Phosphor's stoop just as Phosphor had upon Fogginius'.

Cosima was sweet-smelling, and Pulco basked in her heat as long as she allowed it, for Cosima was like a beach of hot sand. Her stories were often interrupted by Fogginius, who always seemed to know when people were listening with delight to someone else. One imagines:

"Once upon a time," Cosima begins, her arms cradling Pulco to her curiously resonant rotundity, "the garden was full of elves so small that if you put one hundred of them in a saucer and asked them to sing, they'd make less noise than a pinch of salt sprinkled on an onion."

Fogginius appears brandishing an evil-looking appurtenance he has found growing in the kitchen garden and that everyone else recognizes is asparagus. Sharking out Cosima's story and elbowing his way past the cook, he cries:

"Ignorant child! You have confused elves with angels, which everyone knows can ambulate by the thousands up and down the anus of a camel—forgive me but the minions of God are *everywhere*, even in the droppings of hens, and there's no telling where they will show up next beating their blue wings, their blue drums, and blowing their blue horns! Had we ears we could hear them whispering within the spheres dung bugs push about. Don't listen to the wench!" Fogginius pulls Pulco from Cosima's lap by the ear: "She'll fill your head with foo-fah! The truth is that elves and fairies, goblins and such, are flimflammery!"

The cook, feeling pity for the saint's captive audience, brings them sweets in a little dish glazed green.

"Now, there are multiplicitous ways to tell an angel from a devil:"—Fogginius gathers steam—"when a devil steps into water, he ignites. An egg boiled in this water will explode. But should an angel settle on water he will glide like a swan. One of the great delights of Paradise is to see the angels gliding. . . ."

Once, after dark, Cosima set up a magic lantern and showed Pulco the glass slides she had herself painted under Phosphor's direction with stains made of colored wax: butterflies and pigs with wings and scenes of an imagined Orient and other things Phosphor had described for her, such as the serpent Apophis, the giant Typhon, the cosmic egg, and the Speaking Tree; and also the landscapes of her own dreams in which the moon was swallowed by the smoking mouth of a volcano before being spat out again.

To Cosima's surprise, little Pulco was terrified. He believed that the kitchen wall would remember those dancing shadows, would somehow engender them later in the deep of night when he would be alone sleeping beside the hearth. Cosima asked the cook: why was little Pulco so frightened? Sullen and stammering, the cook explained that ever since Señor Fantasma had taken little Pulco to the garden shed, where he had kept him for well over an hour, Pulco was frightened of the dark.

11

The weeks passed. Clay gathered strength for the voyage by curing the soles of his feet with parakeet droppings as Fogginius prescribed; Phosphor screwed spectacles together and polished an adjustable case for the world's first collapsible camera and, made fearless by Cosima's proximity, attempted to acquire an audience with Professor Tardanza's daughter:

> *Should you be so generous as to indulge my small wish, 1 would happily recite a short piece from an expanding work which it is my intention to make longer than Homer's and more to the point. Spanish has the most beautiful words of any language! For example:* pulpo, atizador, calamidad . . . *the most beautiful, yes! And the most terrible!*

The letter was returned unopened. Phosphor was ready to abandon everything, to hurl himself from the highest palm he could find, except that having approached a good-sized tree, and having embraced it with the idea of scaling it, he realized that, although he had seen it done, he had never attempted to climb one himself. Taking a footpath to the crest of a cliff, and looking down at the sea, he considered leaping to the beach below, but recalling the crabs that scuttled back and forth in their own mysterious frenzy of motion, it came to him that a poet's corpse could be badly mutilated and he did not want Professor Tardanza's beautiful daughter to look at his corpse and sicken.

If he were to die a poet's death, to lie entire and pale in a beautiful coffin—that might move her to tears. He imagines her bosom heaving in its lace nest from which she pulls an egg—no! a piece of parchment—a poem! And clutching it with tear-soaked fists sobs: *Aie, aie, aie!* Too late!

Panting in the clutches of an erotic melancholy so intense he could barely breathe, Phosphor pulled an inkpot from his spattered vest, a pen, a roll of parchment, and with bitterness and jealous lust recalled what he had seen that very morning: Professor Tardanza's daughter walking among the trees of the plaza on the arm of a handsome brute named Enrique Saladrigas, a student of Tardanza's and—the pain was great—a poet, too.

Choosing a flat, scarred rock overlooking the sea, Phosphor straddled it with a sigh, and, clutching his inkpot, began to weep. He was undone as much by heresy as by love. Because the woman of his dreams ignored him and worse: that morning when he had unwittingly passed her and Saladrigas in the shadows of the trees (where in the name of Hell was her *duenna?*) he had badly fumbled, dropped his hat, and stepped on it. When with a pounding heart he had, so needlessly, excused himself, *she had laughed!* Her terrible laughter still reverberated in his ears; it rattled and thundered in his brain like the body of a vampire eager to leave its coffin, and it made him wonder if there was any sense to the vast universe at all.

Pressing his parchment to the stone, he dipped his pen into the ink and wrote:

Now it is strange how one can see things from afar and be affected. To be a fantastical eye, like a bird on a stalk.

Next he wrote down those things he saw before him: *spiral cliffs* and *jagged rocks; sink holes* and *knobs.* He wrote:

His beard as unbridled as his heart.

He wrote down a word he liked: *malaria.*

Here he was, a cripple and cross-eyed too, yet clean-featured, his hair and eye both raven black; of sharp wit and disputatious mind, of mild manners, regular in his habits; of good conscience, enamored of the world and its mysteries, regular in his bodily functions; a great inventor, the poet of his age, of fiery heart and an exasperated consciousness, a planet yearning after a planet. If he had believed in God, he might have wondered why his Maker had bothered to make him if only to leave him, as it were, unmade.

Blotting his tear-soaked face with his fist, Nuño Alfa y Omega, known as Phosphor, dipped his pen into the little pot of ink he carried with him everywhere and wrote

ONE LAST POEM TO
PROFESSOR TARDANZA'S DAUGHTER:

> *Your laughter piping through my head*
> *utter strangeness piping through my head*
> *I dare to think I would be better dead*
> *To, at your little dovelike feet,*
> *lie not a little dead . . .*

But before he could complete the poem, he saw Pulco come running toward him down the rocky path. Señor Fantasma would wait no longer. Fogginius had prophesied an auspicious day, and their master was projecting an imminent departure! His little face screwed by the urgency of his mission, Pulco told the poet that he must pack his mule.

The dark thoughts dissipated; the girl's laughter vanished from the poet's brain. At last he would set out upon the Great Work: the entire island caged like a bird and like a blossom held in glass seized within his verse forever and ever.

12

When Phosphor returned to the Big House, the cobbled courtyard reverberated with mules, their tails braided with bells, their saddlebags bulging with bug bombs propelled by compressed air, their faces transformed by the leather visors of his own invention.

Sitting on a yellow mule furnished with a quilted saddle, Fogginius wore black spectacles and a visor equipped with a veil; the ancient wizard looked like a hag in exile from a lunar harem. He also carried a bottle of oil to grease his posterior so that it would not get sore, but as hot peppers had steeped in the oil for weeks—the work of Cosima's imagination—Fogginius, unduly agitated, was to ride in a discomfort he could never put his finger on. They set off beneath a green sky stubbled with clouds.

The evening Fantasma and his party left, Cosima celebrated her autonomy by smashing those didactic dinner plates that had once falsely instructed Fantasma as to the nature of the human species—but first she dropped the terrestrial globe she had been carrying. Next she raided the pantry and, dizzy on sugar, took herself to the garden where she

deeply breathed in the potent scent of the spices growing
there. What a relief to be free of the husband she hated and
of that hydraulic marvel: Fogginius' mouth!

Mistress of everything, Cosima high-stepped through the
mansion's silent rooms imagining Fantasma slowly sinking
in quicksand as he screamed. And, because she believed in
magic, and because little Pulco's terror had seeded the idea
in her brain, she painted his image on glass. That night, after
the cook had gone to bed, she projected this image upon the
kitchen wall. Freckled with grease from the cook's deep-fry-
ing, Fantasma agonized till midnight as Cosima finished off
a six-egg flan and paired her nails.

(This image, numbered 803, I found among the ocularscopic slides. It is larger than the others and vibrantly
colored. Cosima was not an especially gifted artist, but
Fantasma is recognizable and his expression of grief and
terror as he is about to be swallowed whole is remarkable.)

The next morning, Cosima, having slept late and leisurely bathed in a precious room shimmering with glass,
took herself to the balcony to comb her wet hair in the sun.
The balcony was richly curtained with vines; naked, yet
concealed, Cosima gazed at the landscape, which dropped
dramatically to the sea, and saw blazing upon the creamy
beach a city of fortune she knew had not been there the
night before. Running to the kitchen, she bade the cook
descend the hill at once to discover her vision's meaning.

"It cannot be a mirage," Cosima said, "because I can
perceive people milling about down there—although they
are no bigger than ants!"

Breathless and agitated, the cook returned an hour later
with the news that pirates had organized a thieves' market
of such luxury no one thought to complain, and everyone,

including the authorities, were down there now, benefiting from the loot which included the latest in French fashion, priceless jewels to be had for a kiss, pocket astrolabes she thought had something to do with witchcraft, velvet shoes, copal, wine. . . . Shyly she held up a gold locket and blushed.

This city, its tents made of sail and boutiques of bamboo and colored rags, was lorded over by a pirate prince—and who knows where he had learned to swagger with such irresistible charm, to braid his mustaches into his mane, and to speak convincingly about just about anything? Where had he learned to laugh with such felicity the moon would lose its bearings each time a thing amused him? How was it that he could seize a woman with his gaze and gather her body after, like a fruit set out on a plate?

Having heard enough, Cosima dressed herself in a sumptuous scarlet gown that had long ago done nothing for Fantasma's grandmother but in which she looked just as Helen might have looked for Faust, and taking up a banana leaf to shield her pretty eyes from the sun, hurried down to the pirate souk.

13

But what about our party of travelers? As Phosphor's mule passed through Fantasma's gate and stumbled forth upon the cobbled way, the terrific implications of what he was about to do overwhelmed his brain. It came to him that he must thrust a series of stanzas in assonance into the very entrails of his epic—stanzas comprised of wind zones and ocean currents, the names of inland waters, descriptions of useful products, of the climate, too; and volcanoes and river systems. He would determine and disclose the action of waves upon the sandstone coasts, the temperatures of sub-terranean lakes. He would chronicle the premonitory signs of earthquakes, the force of waves, the height of tides, the sound of winds, the smell of medicinal springs. He would evoke caverns lucent of carbonate of lime, whirlpools and waterspouts; rainbows, meteors, mirages, and will-o'-the-wisps. Not only would he be his island's first poet laure-ate and photographer, he would be its first geographer and cartographer! His endeavor was greater than epic: it was encyclopedic!

And all this in honor of Professor Tardanza's daughter. He imagined her stupefication the moment he would lay the entire island at her feet. (No wonder, dear Ved, that Ombos refers to Nuño Alfa y Omega as "Birdland's Diderot.")

But, from the start, Fogginius proved himself highly disruptive of projects grounded in revery. Only Fantasma—whom the scholar continued to fascinate and whose tuft of red hair now blazed an incongruous trail—was not put out of temper. Fogginius was forever dismounting to investigate a donkey's dropping, to badger a nursing mother for a little milk, to scrape the foam from the mouth of a soldier's horse, to examine the hindmost part of Phosphor's mule in order to fix his mind on the eye of the wind and hence foretell the weather.

When at last they had left the trees along the town road behind them and were embraced by a savage path enfevered by scarlet oleander, the saint took it into his crazed head that he would enliven the aboriginal way and astonish his companions with the knowledge he had accumulated over the years. True to himself, he did not ask if they might prefer to enjoy the beauties of the day in silence, but, setting his mouth in motion, began to discourse, unstoppable, on *miracula*: double eggs and bezoars and hair balls; how once he had found a minuscule and thinking brain within a cherry stone, and where one could procure cutlery for dwarfs and giants.

Just then Professor Tardanza and his daughter appeared riding together in the opposite direction. They had been gathering flowering branches in the woods, and the young girl, astride a horse the color of butter, was wreathed in blossoms. So tightly was the poet's heart squeezed with longing that had it been a lime, seeds would have bulleted from his ears.

When the girl and her father rode past, Phosphor offered his most lovesick look, a look of such intensity that had

Fogginius remained silent she might have been moved. But the scholar opened his trap:

"The best remedy against lightning is to wear one's turds—dried and sewn with a piece of silk—against the heart. The turd is dry, corrupt, combustible, commemorative, and at best, cumuliform—"

Professor Tardanza did not nod, nor tip his hat, but spurred his own horse on, frowning, as if to say: *I do not approve of the company you keep.*

"That girl who just passed!" Fogginius spluttered with ill-founded enthusiasm, "has offended some pagan deity and is being transformed to shrubbery before our eyes! Soon she will tumble from her steed and take root by the way-side. . . . I would never have believed it had I not seen it with my own eyes!" For an instant he shut up, marveling.

But Phosphor did not hear him. He who never prayed was praying that a meteor would strike Fogginius dead where he sat. And although they had only just left the city of Pope Publius behind and had been journeying but an hour, Phosphor was submerged in weariness.

The day died. Fogginius was silent only when catching his breath. When the party stopped and Clay set about to roast those things he had brained for their supper, Fogginius described procedures for the procuration of corpses, both fresh and moldering, and methods of dissection both ancient and new—thereby vanquishing everyone's appetite but his own. Cracking a baked egg against his bony knee, he entertained them with a catalog of distinctions between angels, archangels, and archons, and wondered if all had microscopic or telescopic vision, or both—or neither, but instead of a type surnatural and thus inconceivable.

As Fogginius spoke and Fantasma listened in rapture, Phosphor pondered why his master cherished the saint's advice and admired his mind so much that he—who was going broke—had been paying him to think. With much gnashing of teeth, Phosphor recalled his stepfather's incessant punishments, the insane blandishments that had rained unfailingly down upon him when he was a boy: the times he had been constrained to wear a live lizard in his breeches, to chew sand, to eat a stew of snails cooked in their own glue. Kicking out the fire, Clay too fantasized of reducing the saint to a pulp. Pulco, however, appeared content as he cleared the supper things and scrubbed a pan—he had plugged his ears with a paste of bread, moistened with saliva.

"The black man is black"—detonating, Fogginius threw himself upon his hammock—"because he burns from within with such intensity all his whiteness has been consumed. The red man burns with less heat; the yellow—" Suddenly the world was silent.

Silent. As if a great lid of lead had been lowered from the top of the sky. Fogginius had fallen asleep, as had small Pulco and the mules. This silence was so exquisite and so dense that the poet attempted to capture it in verse. He wrote:

> *A silence like a blotter soft and thick*
> *Soaks up the forest's ink*
> *Allowing me to dream and think*

Phosphor put down his pen and, gazing up at the wheeling sky, invoked in one breath the Mother of Heaven, Venus, and Professor Tardanza's daughter. Within moments he was fast asleep—as were the others, strung from trees like figs.

In his dream, Phosphor saw Professor Tardanza's daughter threading toward him as naked as a thing of Eden. Opening his arms to receive her, he pushed his feet deep into the nebulous mud upon which he was precariously standing, to keep from falling.

She was hot. Before he touched her, he could feel how the air about her burned: she was poised at the center of a mandorla of fire. But just as he would embrace her, his rival Enrique Saladrigas slipped between them, and Phosphor was eclipsed by a body twice as tall and twice as broad as he. In despair he battered at his rival's back with both his fists and at the buttocks that now pressed against his face so that he could barely breathe. A terrific stench was upon the poet now, and the more he battered Saladrigas, the greater his rival grew.

And Phosphor was in the embrace of an outsize octopus; its antediluvian face pressed down upon his own. With a cry the poet tore his mouth from the creature's beak, and looking to the sky saw with clarity, luminous against the ink of night, the constellation of the skeleton.

The poet screamed. Waking, he found that something still pinned him down. It was Fogginius. Fogginius, whose dreadful testicles, so like the desiccated things he chose to carry close to his heart to conjure evil fortune, forced the poet's lips. Revulsed nearly to madness, Phosphor bit the saint fiercely, and Fogginius, leaping to the ground, began to shout. With loathing and amazement, and just as the sun appeared foaming upon the horizon, Phosphor listened to the saint's breathless explanation:

"A cure! For rheumatism! To sit upon a poet's face at dawn!" And: "I am cured!" Fogginius tottered and lurched about in the morning dew, arousing the many green apes drowsing in the tree-tops. Hurled into consciousness, they responded by screeching, precipitating a million birds into the scarlet sky—those birds that in distant days before pesticides filled the woods with their hot, palpitating bodies, their voices like bells, the philosophical stones of their eggs.

14

Phosphor's chronic melancholia had deepened to despondency. His dream's sad implication, the rude awakening, illuminated the comfortless state of his love life. Looking back in time to the moment when with a lingering moan love had first flowered in his breast, reviewing each affair up to the present, he thought that never, not once, had he won his heart's desire, known a maiden's timid tremor, the delights of reciprocal attraction. Monsters of will, his mistresses had always chosen him. From the first kiss, disappointment had flagged him down.

With a shudder, Phosphor recalled the titanic vigor of his mistresses' constitutions, their iron-clad affection, the stern, fixed stare of their lust, the fearfully earnest letters he received with terror; how faithfully they punished his evasions, the silent thunderbolts of their angry looks, the purposed damage they invariably inflicted upon his reputation when, at last, he made his escape.

The second day of their journey, Phosphor made a vow. If upon his return he could not within a week win the professor's daughter, he would abandon the ocularscopic project and all other inventing and devote himself, body and soul, to poetry. He would no more clutter the universe with things but animate it with verses, dreamed in silence and in silence pressed to parchment.

He imagined himself desiccated and hollow—like a pod devoid of seed—but with a great burning body of work growing beneath his frantic pen. He would devote himself tirelessly to the epic at hand. A monument of buried pain, he would be famous beyond belief, so famous that a day would not go by without Professor Tardanza's daughter hearing his name. In school, her children would be made to memorize his verse; the queen of Spain herself would sail to Birdland solely to hold Phosphor's hand.

But here the revery takes a perilous turn. It seems the queen cannot, will not, let go of the poet's frail hand.

"Poetry," she breathes, "is the lubrication for life's frictions." Dreadfully sovereign, as fixed as a polar cap, she ignores his mute appeal, treads upon his feet, barks in his ear that the poet is a cog of God, and with a seismic shudder insists that he be equal to her Great Occasion.

❦

Late that afternoon, the road—in truth a protohistoric path, tortuous and precipitous—vanished altogether. Spying a dejectus in the grass, Fogginius dismounted to see whither it pointed. The turd led them to the lip of a chasm at the foot of which the sea had hollowed a whirlpool—*an eager mouth*, the poet thought, *entreating them, in savage tongue, to leap.*[*]

---

[*] Writes Ombos: *If in Lilliput Gulliver's mouth and anus are equally visible, in Brobdingnag Gulliver as Nanunculus is more a mouth, the suckling of nurse, frolicsome handmaiden, and mischievous monkey whose perilous nursing brings to mind King Kong's abduction of Fay Wray. Nuño Alfa y Omega foreshadows this vision with the lines:*

Too tired to turn back, they set themselves down for an early supper. As Clay built a fire and little Pulco set to dressing a company of birds the thug had throttled, Phosphor unpacked his tripod and his black box to capture the whirlpool forever with silver nitrate on glass. He trembled so close to the land's edge; the sight of so deep a pit flooded his soul's chambers with dread.

It was decided that while waiting for their food, they would play a game of lotto. From his saddlebags, Yahoo Clay pulled the box of painted cards that showed all manner of things: flying fish, the fortifications of Pope Publius, the garrote, the guanabana, and the coconut; a poultry seller, a water peddler, a milkman and his mules; the pyramid of Cheops, the Holy Mother, the Great Cathedral of Oaxaca, the wounds of Christ; a fig, a banana, and a parakeet—a game so subverted by Fogginius that by the time it was over, tempers were badly frayed. The cards called forth all sorts of associations and Fogginius could not help but recall recipes and riddles and curious customs and ceremonial sacrifices: the witch trials raging in Europe, red hens and peacocks shrilling warning of tigers ravening in woods, miasmatic infections, focusing instruments and paradoxes; how so-and-so had found gold in a graveyard that looked exactly like human teeth, how the monks of India smear their faces with dung, how lepers would be kings and how the jews killed Jesus; the burning of the Albigenses at Montségur.

Phosphor, who, like Pulco, had taken to living with bread in his ears, missed all this; he did not hear when Clay cried *Completo!* and so could not know that the game

---

Poetry catches in my maw
like the breast of Time.
I suckle Death.

was over. This caused confusion, a quarrel, and a string of complaints during which Clay accused the poet of cheating and incivility. Oblivious to the upset he had himself caused, Fogginius gaily pointed out the prodigious vegetative power of the wood, naming the many purges and poisons he recognized—

"To stick in your epic, dear poet!" he beamed at Phosphor. "Proof that I have liberally forgiven you the nasty bite you gave me this morning!"

Then, grabbing Señor Fantasma by the sleeve, he postulated that the chimerical unhealthiness of the climate, its fickle temperatures, and the spontaneous alterations of its air convinced him they would be assailed that night by uncommon swarms of flies, gnats, moths, animalcules, and other calamities invisible to the naked eye.

"We must sleep under nets else be plagued by troublesome bites, inflammations, noxious exhalations, and velocity of the blood." He assured Fantasma—who was weighted down with silver amulets—that he had brought with him mercurial purges, a gaggle of borax, Armenian bole in vinegar, and fungal ash. However, he would hate to have to part with any of it so soon. He insisted upon the nets else they all harvest fatality. As for himself, he would not sleep unless a net were provided; nor did he wish to see his poor friend the poet assailed by vampire moths. It is fortunate that Fogginius was nearly blind, for his stepson was able to provide him with a fictive net. This Pulco draped over and above the saint who, prostrate and tightly bandaged in his blanket, was ready to sleep. Fogginius promised in a soft gurgle that he would not stir the whole night through—else tear the precious net.

As Fogginius trumpeted and wheezed, Clay offered to

toss him into the precipice. But Phosphor hated violence, and revealed the central role Fogginius had played in his life.

"I'll find a way to gag him," he promised Clay. "I might manage to convince him that to use the vocal cords is unnatural—the proof being that his throat is always sore—and create for his own use a language of sand, of straw, of dust. I'll *invent* something—a muffler, a word snare, a stifler. Somehow or other I'll knot the old stinker's tongue."

Later, his ears stuffed with wild parsley, Phosphor lay gazing at the sky. Long after midnight he fell asleep—a leaky vessel upon an agitated ocean.

15

For two days Fango Fantasma had been silent. Indeed, Fogginius' conversation was so congested, infrangible, and dense that, had he wanted to, Fantasma would have been hard pressed to stick a word in, even edgewise. However, Fantasma shared Phosphor's baleful propensity and was not eager to talk. He had fallen to staring at his own reflection in a pocket mirror—not from vanity as might be supposed, but to reassure himself that he was still there. The farther away he went from familiar things, the more fragmented and permeable he felt himself to be—and the more haunted. The woods, the sea, the sky, the relic path under his mule's vanishing feet appeared to percolate to transparency.

Fantasma's unstable state of mind had been precipitated by a worsening pecuniary crisis. For several years he had hounded the papal authorities for permission to import Africans to work his mines and plantations. When at last his wish had been granted, he spent the lion's part of his languishing fortune to build and equip a ship, which, upon its return from Africa, its cargo chained and bolted to the hold, had been made to vanish—perhaps by those evil spirits that had plagued his line for three generations. It seemed to Fantasma, as the very clouds appeared to plot against him overhead, that he and his family had always been the playthings of witches.

Fogginius had once told Señor Fantasma that at the world's edge lived a people born riddled with holes. This peculiar race amused themselves by plugging their perforations with sod and planting them with roses.

"More often than not the wedding night ends in disaster," Fogginius told Fantasma, "for in their frenzied state the lovers—decked head to foot in thorny briars—tear one another to shreds."

"Such is the way of love—" Phosphor, eavesdropping, was cut to the quick by the story. He made up a little list of rhymes to keep for later: thorn/sworn, latch/patch, fur/burr, thistle/whistle.*

This night Fantasma felt like a sieve man; he felt that his substance was seeping out through the pores of his skin. To make matters worse, their finger of rock above the whirlpool—if certified by an auspicious dropping—was possibly haunted. Certain signs—caricatural boles and an abandoned wasp's nest—implied that they had tied their hammocks between what had once been sacred trees.

As their fire died, Fantasma stretched and, pulling on his fingers one by one until they popped, thought about

---

* *The descent into the female vortex is vertiginous,* writes Ombos, *and culminates in the revelation of that* vile machine, *that* reeking chest; *Celia's own* Pandora's Box: *her chamber pot—which, as Groddeck has pointed out, when stained with menstrual blood, is for the little boy an emblem of castration—or rather, the proof that the female is a castrated male. Celia's chamber pot, like the Brobdingnagian wench's vulva, is a metaphor for the Medusa herself.* This cave . . . this gulph insatiable . . . *the sight that turns a man to stone. It is no accident that the Nanunculus' intimate view of a frolicsome girl's outsiged cabinet—a mirror of his own incapacities—is followed by the sight of a decapitation which in a fit of lyricism Gulliver likens to the* jet d'eau *of* Versailles: *an extravagant ejaculation, to say the very least.*

Phosphor's ocularscope. He imagined himself enthroned upon a velvet chair, turning a crank that would yield up the island image after image.

Too agitated to sleep, Fantasma told himself the story of the nun who had neglected to cross herself before eating a banana. That failing, he attempted to bring to mind the tender moments of his infancy, but could only recall those family stories that, since cognizance, profoundly distressed him. Stories of those unstable ghosts taking root, tall as trees, in the dining room, causing the roast beef to explode; hovering near the birthing chair whenever a Fantasma was born, to snap up the umbilical cord the instant it was cut.

And then Fantasma thought he heard his own cord, and the cords of his forefathers, being pulled along the ground. He moaned and clutched his balls in terror; above the roar of the whirlpool, he heard one thousand phantoms stepping among the stones and breathed an air thick with the smoke of one thousand cigars.

Fantasma shivered. A clammy air rose up from under him; it mouthed his bones and caused his teeth to hammer. When the moon's thin wafer pulled itself up over the horizon, he peered timidly out from under his blanket, thinking to catch a glimpse of the ghosts that—he could hear them distinctly—were spooking the campsite. What he saw caused him to scream with such conviction the others were wrenched from sleep to see that the world beneath was no longer solid but palpitating with hundreds of thousands of frogs. The indigenous population had called the place above the whirlpool *Tlöck*. Indeed, as the frogs advanced snapping gnats, the party heard distinctly the percussive sound of their feasting: *Tlöck, tlöck, tlöck.*

Transfixed with terror, Fantasma sailed that amphibious

sea howling as Yahoo Clay, more naked than any ape, waded among the little red and gold and green bodies, battering them with a club. Phosphor sat transfixed, Pulco wept, and Fogginius beat the air and cried:

"The magic is severe! My net's dissolved!" And then: "A dream! A dream and an oracle! We must count them!" The saint dropped to the ground and, fumbling among the frogs, raved: "Fallen from the sky! Clay! Desist! You are smattering the brains of rational angels!"

They finished the night prostrate but wakeful. It seemed to them that the entire cosmos reeked of mildew, stagnant pools, the shit of fish, the saliva of snakes, and the sulfurous flatulence of saints. Sometime before dawn, the frogs vanished into thin air—supporting Fogginius' thesis.

Ved, surely you recall a red tower, freakish and austere; built of a bloody marble imported from Spain, it shadows a squalid corner of the Old Quarter. Here Rais Secundo, his piles perpetually festering, gnawed his knuckles and plotted a world as seamless and silent as a saucer. His chamber, too, was of marble and perfectly round. (Secundo feared corners, shadows, and recesses of any kind.) This chamber brings to mind a tomb, and according to the tourist guide should be seen at midnight. In that ghostly hour, the place reeks of ill fortune. And although the Church can no longer claim the authority it had in Secundo's time, still the adjacent cathedral contains more gold than the wealth of all the island brought together, its gutters more copper and its treasure-house more silver, pearls, and brocade. (Yet the priest continues to panhandle after hard cash, badgering his flock—fisherfolk, mostly, weavers and such who worship in rags.)

What I'm getting at is this: the very week Fantasma and his party set off to seize the island by necromancy, Rais Secundo called a meeting of the Doctors of the Church and his Inquisitional Officers to discuss urgent matters. This list was long. He was hot after smoke and itching for pyres; he craved the stench of sinners roasting.*

Now, it was assumed by the Powers that if the Christ had both masticated and swallowed, *he did not digest.* Once food hit Christ's stomach it vaporized like water on hot coals. But several days before the departure, as he sat beside Yahoo Clay jabbering deep into the night, Fogginius perfected the argument that Christ produced an excrement in every way like that of every man. Later, in the streets and marketplace, he labored his conviction to all who would listen and was heard by Secundo's infallible spies.

Fogginius' argument went like this: if God gave his son a physical body the better to punish him, surely that body which—it was documented—bled and perspired—digested, too. Fogginius had himself seen the Lord's foreskin in Barcelona under glass. He reasoned: if the Lord had a virile member, he surely urinated; if he urinated, surely he shat. And did that not prove excrement was a good, a natural thing? So necessary in gardens and love potions alike?

This abominable argument was overheard by three shuddering and credible witnesses. Fogginius' abandoned hovel, its floor a rampart of clumped and rotted things, was visited by Rais Secundo himself. He came back with an awful look in his eyes and described the hole as hot with heresy and as pagan as an African bazaar overrun with devils black and

---

* According to Ombos, once the Church had created a Hell of roaring flames, it was inevitable it would then set about roasting sinners on earth—an imagined Hell the inspiration and the justification.

brown.

He had the place spattered with holy salt and then he set it on fire.

According to the records, so many devils perished in that fire they left a pool of rancid butter thirty feet across and three thumbs deep. This butter was collected, filtered, poured into blue bottles, and kept as proof of sorcery. Awaiting the wizard's capture, Secundo arranged the bottles on his windowsill where, against the day, they cast blue reflections. Toying with his deadly instruments impatiently, Secundo bitterly complained: "All the pins and thumbscrews in God's universe can't nail a witch who has flown the coop!" These infamous words were taken up by children:

> *Thumbscrew, thumbscrew*
> *Ducking stool.*
> *Bleed sir, bleed sir,*
> *Buckets full.*

and

> *Pin and pillory*
> *Gibbet and noose,*
> *Catch the witches*
> *As they roost.*
> *If they wake and fly away,*
> *Roast them on another day.*

The blue bottles were said to have a weird influence on those who saw them. A novitiate of the Order of Rosy Water was quietly conversing with the Inquisitor in his tower when he was suddenly seized in the fist of a fit and sent a piping pot of tea into Secundo's lap.

16

One of the most curious exhibits on view in the National Museum is a preserved lôplôp skin—headless. It has called forth many fanciful conjectures within the impassioned scholarly community worldwide. A lôplôp's skull has never been found, although beaks, numbered and labeled, are shelved in profusion—once a cumbersome currency. The beak—with which the lôplôp dug for clams and pulled itself up vertical sea walls—weighs anywhere from fifty to seventy-five pounds. A sumptuous tangerine color, it is very like ivory and dramatically hooked. In order to walk without wounding its own abdomen, surely the great bird had to walk with its head thrown back.

The lôplôp skin is displayed stretched taut upon a wooden frame; the vestigial wings are secured and splayed, the tufted tail hangs free. Even without its head the lôplôp is the size of a mature black bear. Because the creature's genitals are visible—an unusual phenomenon in birds—a cloth has been knotted about its loins, making the lôplôp appear simultaneously human and crucified.

The lôplôp's feathers, if close and thick—very like fur— are not beautiful. The natives made blankets of the skins and served ceremonial feasts of shellfish and fritters and yams in their beaks. They did not eat the bird's flesh because the lôplôp sounded human when it screamed, and when captured begged for mercy on its knees in a melodious language our own Hildegard von Pfeffertits suggests may have sounded like classical Arabic interpreted on an oboe. And so it seems the lôplôp was killed for blankets and serving platters and its flayed corpse taken out to sea and dumped where the tides and the crabs made the best of its flesh and its bones. This explains why no skeleton has ever been found, nor a skull; the riddle of the creature's head remains unsolved. By the time Señor Fantasma and his party set out upon their journey, no lôplôp had been seen for decades, and indeed, had there been no beaks to prove it had once enlivened the coasts by the thousands, the lôplôp would have joined the phoenix and the roc on a mythic list, or worse, vanished from the minds of men.

❦

Awaking before the others, Phosphor lay in his hammock relishing the moment. It occurred to him that the lôplôp must have a place in his epic; indeed, it was evident he could not do the island justice without reference to its fauna and native population. With little difficulty he recalled the ancient refrain with which Fantasma's cook had coaxed little Pulco to sleep when upon a stormy evening the child was especially haunted by whatever happened to him alone with Fantasma in the garden shed. An ancient song, he did not doubt; in other words, *authentic*. Phosphor considered that by including the song in his epic, he would revolutionize the genre and assure the esteem of Professor Tardanza.

A precarious procedure ensued—the poet sitting in the hammock and setting the uncorked bottle of ink between his thighs, all the while propping up the writing book with his knees. But soon he was covering the page with his elegant scrawl, marveling how fresh the poem looked with the aboriginal addition; how it enlivened the poem and the page. With a thrill known only to innovators he read:

Although it is heavy, tenderly I carry the beak,
Tenderly I carry the beak to the house of my intended.
To the house of my beloved, I carry the beak
The ceremonial beak, the sacred beak
To serve the wedding fritters, o lôplôp, yes!
Yah! Yah! Yah!

And my intended calls out, calls out
from behind her father's door:
"Oh my beloved, my intended, is that you with the beak?
Bring it quickly! Bring it now, quickly through the door!
For the fritters are already in the oil!
Yah! The fragrant fritters!"

And my beloved's father, my intended's mother
call out from behind the door:
"Is it an estimable beak you bring us?
The shape and color of the waning moon?
We want only the best for our daughter!
A beak as white as the moon!"

So! I strike at the door of my beloved's house
And the door opens. I smell cooking
          I smell the fritters cooking.

And my beloved cries:
"Let the wedding feast begin!
Oh yes! Yah! Yah! Yah!
For my mother, father, sisters, and brothers,
Aunts, uncles, and all my ancestors are hungry!!
YAH!"

After breakfast (which was prepared by Clay and served by little Pulco) Fantasma and his party left the enchanted precipice. This time, as they ambled through the clotted trees, they saw not only the turd that had marked their path the previous evening, but a large stone squatting among the wild pineapples and orchids. Approaching with misgiving, his man Clay beside him, Fantasma suddenly veered away and as with terror and disgust he retched into the shrubbery, the others saw the hateful thing in its entirety, its face riddled with fractures, its privates bearded with moss: a monumental frog perpetually positioned for sexual intercourse.*

"Had we only seen this yesterday!" the poet sighed, "we'd have spent the night elsewhere." Little Pulco slipped from his mule and before anyone could stop him climbed atop the totem—he was, you will recall, but a child. For this he was severely admonished by Fogginius and sent scrambling

---

* The surprising treatment of the curious and mystic frog (preserved in the museum's tea garden—a favorite haunt of mine with its rare blossoms, frog pond, and rookery) brings to mind those gigantic heads recently discovered in Mexico, although the frog is playfully sexual and the heads horribly grim. They express—as does all Olmec statuary—acute melancholy. Not surprising when one considers that the Olmec spent their first weeks immobilized, their feet in the air and their little skulls compressed by boards! I imagine that like the emblematic jaguar, these infants were adept at roaring. As you know, the Olmec vanished precipitously; my theory is that acute rage caused them to self-destruct.

On the other hand, the aboriginal infants of Birdland learned to roar only after they had been either reduced to slavery or fed to Fantasma's hounds. After a brief decade of terror, they were reduced to silence, a hush that has now given way to fearful pictures in the mind and a new awareness of all that was once here and is now lost.

back to his mule.

"The universe is a place of infinite wonders," Fogginius began to lecture as soon as the party set off again, "wherein angels may appear to mortals in the guise of lowly brachiopods, wherein the cosmic script may be deciphered in the stench of pigs and the minute voices of flies. Could we but decipher those particles of suchness, we would be far closer to God than we are at present. Nothing is lowly," the saint addressed Pulco, whose feelings he had hurt, "and sacred images are not to be taken for hobbyhorses. Beware the seductions of this world; purge yourself with clay each Saturday; prick your foreskin with a nice sharp thorn whenever you feel naughty, and you will make an old man very proud of you."

Reaching out to give the boy's head an affectionate tousle, Fogginius tumbled from his mule with the sound of a great many coconuts falling down a flight of stairs. No bones were broken, but he was badly bruised about the head, elbows, buttocks, and knees. The party was held up for an hour while little Pulco rubbed the sore spots with a noxious salve from an oily tin the saint kept tied to his saddle with a quantity of rotten string.

Meanwhile, the poet dreamed beside a clump of odoriferous orchids and, gazing at the sky, was visited with inspiration: the sacred frog could be used in the poem as an emblem of some kind, perhaps a metaphor for his undying love for Professor Tardanza's daughter. Although the stone was shaggy and badly pocked, its overall shape was still recognizable, "as my own heart will be," he thought, "upon my return. Although I shall suffer at the hands of Time, my face wrinkle, and my shoulders stoop, still my heart shall keep its shape."

Phosphor asked Pulco to draw for him a picture of a heart and a frog side by side to illustrate his point:

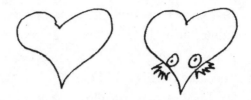

(Pulco's little sketch is one of the many curiosities on display
at the National Library.) So enthralled was the poet as he
watched little Pulco laboring away that he was much startled when Fogginius, who had been standing quietly above
them both for several minutes, broke the silence and said:

"Ah! You have noticed how closely the frog's statue resem-
bles the human heart! It is because the frog was the aboriginal emblem of love. They admired its abundance of eggs, the
phallic shape of its tads." He paused then. "A pagan thing.
I, sure as shit, have no need for it."

The poet recalled that the natives of Birdland had admired
the taste of raw shellfish, the blatantly sexual appearance of
certain mollusks, tubers, and blossoms—as much as the
phallic beak of the lôplôp. He waited for the sun to illuminate the spot, and then captured the idol's image on glass.
Fantasma approached, then approvingly said:

"Incomprehensible things are horrible by their natures
and would thus attempt to escape us. Some things are like
water—most things, in fact, and cannot be kept from pour-
ing into one ear and out the other. The head is full of holes,
after all. But now the thing is mine! New conquests each
day. . . ." He wandered off.

Phosphor, fearing Fantasma's mind was indeed becoming porous, shivered. A sensitive man, the idea that a mind
could be thought of as porous unsettled him—even if the
image was his own. *Of course,* he thought, *such is the risk of
listening to Fogginius hour after hour. Look what has happened*

to Yahoo Clay. Once he was merely a thug. Now he is a maniac.
(Clay was, at that instant, pulling the wings from several
scarlet and indigo butterflies he had captured with his hat.)

"Stop your ears!" Phosphor cried out to little Pulco, suddenly concerned that the child's mind, already strange, be
addled further. But Pulco, who had no need of such advice,
did not hear him.

❧

Ved, in your last letter you asked for a "view" of Pinhole
Lagoon. I write this sitting on the sandbank that continues
to divide the lagoon from the sea. To the left there is a break
in the clouds that, illuminated from behind, offers a pale
apricot sky studded with white cirro-macula and looking
like the inner shell of the Pinhole oyster—the same colors,
the same pearly brilliance.

Mountains mark the horizon and in places meld with
the sky; beneath the hills rise a deeply mysterious green
except there, where the cliffs are the color of bone. Upon the
opposite bank, twenty palms rise in silhouette. The lagoon
stretches before me—just as you remember; all is still but for
the sky transforming slowly, and the pounding surf behind.
I've not heard a cormorant oink for an hour.

Now if I took my little boat across the water to the edge
of the lagoon, I would see birds, the birds of Birdland everywhere—the flocks of spoonbills and ibis sitting in the trees,
settling down for the evening, and the pelicans too, heading
silently toward their nests for the night. The trees are rus-
tling with infant herons.

The air is fragrant. It is a nourishing air and bracing.
Breathing in Birdland is a little like biting into a sweet lime.

17

As the dust of the road thickened to mud—for the rainy season had just begun—Señor Fantasma and his party continued on through uncharted country—a steaming breach in which midges and serpents proliferated. Armed with a large stick, little Pulco beat the path as Yahoo Clay fired musket balls into the undergrowth with the intention to destroy whatever happened to be there.

"It is a thing paradoxically strange," Fogginius panted, nearly in tears, "that the Holy Father, adorably great and wise, has provided the world with nuisances. You ask *why*," Fogginius continued to himself (for the others had secured their ears with bread), "why God, in all His Rectorial Supereminence and Capacity, wormholed these woods with perils and pests. Listen well; here is the answer:

"Firstly, by creating things noxious, hideous, and wild, God reveals that His capacities are infinite, and that He will not be bound by beauty, nor by common sense. He chooses to be illogical and create things with stingers and fangs, the color green, mucosities, the polar regions, ejaculations, the disfigured races of fishes, fevers, frenzies, and rotten eggs—why? To keep us on our toes! Anxiety is the Sublime

Educator! Anxiety, fellow pilgrims, is the Gateway to Grace. Anxiety and . . . Terror!"

Lost in thought, Señor Fantasma, his sable eyes ignited by greed, appreciated an imposing number of rare cabinet woods thickening in the gloom, and he imagined his retinue swelled by a multitude of vassals wielding saws and hatchets.

"I am pondering," Fogginius said, as if reading Fantasma's thoughts, "how many Africans with hatchets it would take to raze this pernicious place of nastiness." But Phosphor, dreaming of love, was enthralled by the forest's flaming beauty. He noted with delight parrots the size of thumbs and the color of old orange peel, conversing—he was certain—in their multitudes among roses as large as his own palpitating heart.

I am now penetrating, he scribbled with inky fingers on a stained scrap of parchment, *with joy and terror, the Eternal Feminine: moist, mossy, hidden, nameless. I hurry into darkness.* In the margin he penned *nameless/darkness.* The rhyme would serve him later.

That afternoon the forest gave way to stunted pineapples swarming with wasps. They came to a perniciously weeded meadow stretching to the land's end—a jumbled embankment of volcanic rubble, black sand, and foaming sea. In the center of the meadow a gigantic bobadilla—named after the first European to see one—scintillated in the sun and bathed the scorched grasses in promising shadows.

Fantasma, whose stomach had been growling for an hour, ordered his man Yahoo to wade into the bay—but a league away—to gather sea cucumbers for soup, and spiny lobsters, and the pink ovaries of sea urchins to be prepared with the simples Fogginius would gather and Pulco would season with pepper, vinegar, and oil.

"Take these to the bobadilla you see yonder," Fantasma said. "There we will be waiting."

"Beware of mirages in the air," Fogginius extolled the thug as he set off, "and prickly things underfoot. Come, my little paradise," he called to Pulco, "let us gather greens together." But little Pulco began to cry and refused to follow the saint "who," he confided to Phosphor, "would gather greens in my bum."

"Well, then," Phosphor proposed, "run after Yahoo Clay and help him pry some mussels from the rocks."

"My greens aren't safe with him neither." Pulco refused to budge.

"You follow Yahoo Clay!" Fantasma barked, and offered to give Pulco a kick. "Else I split you in two. Since when do children have voices?" Crestfallen, the boy followed the monster, but at a distance, and dragging his feet.

Clucking to their mules, Phosphor and Fantasma descended an incline tufted with scree, and approaching the bobadilla saw that its branches were hung with a startling collection of barber's basins. A path appeared—smoothly laid and imbedded with minute white and yellow stones Fantasma recognized at once to be teeth. He feared they had entered a country of cannibals and was about to turn and flee when a barber, his bald head waxed to a high shine, leapt down from the tree in his apron.

"Welcome to the only arboreal barbershop in the universe," he bowed, "which is also a shrine to our Holy Mother." A second look revealed the tree was hung with votive presents as well as basins: canes and crutches, hearing trumpets, tin ears, wax hearts, tin buttocks, viscera of brass. Candles stuck to dirty saucers burned in such profusion in the lurid, teeming tree that the air smelled of hot tallow. A plain wooden chair had been secured between the branches; it faced a large mirror, above which balanced a Virgin of painted lead. She swung on a pivot in the breeze, twinkling in and out of the leaves much as a figure on a beloved barometer Phosphor had left behind on a shelf. He found himself wistfully dreaming of home when, with surprise, he noticed the Virgin held no infant in her arms but instead a formidable pair of pliers.

" . . . And I pull teeth." The barber beamed and pointed to the path.

The sun was bright, the meadow cheerful, the barber engaging. While Fogginius busied himself among the bushes and as Phosphor uncorked his ink, Señor Fantasma climbed into the tree.

"My head and beard do prosecute me," he complained, "so I beg you to begin at once with an energetic lathering and scraping." As the barber prepared to refresh his face, Fantasma asked him to tell the story of how he came to set up shop in such an unlikely place. "My ears have been cruelly belabored by the saint you can perceive yonder gathering lettuce. So potent are his words that they melt wax; it is impossible to escape him. I would have you purge his babble with your own."

"It is well that you ask me to lather you up and to speak simultaneously," said the barber, "as I can speak only when my hands are occupied. I speak to the rhythm of my scissors and my razor; I speak to the rhythm of scrapings and sudsings; and should you need a tooth pulled, I'll speak to the rhythm of my pliers."

"I like that!" cried the poet from under the tree, "and I've written it down."

"You have seen the pathway paved with molars," the

barber went on; "the idea was not mine but the Virgin Mary's, come to me in a dream."

"I've no tooth to be pulled," said Fantasma with haste. "But my head and beard are driving me insane."

"I prefer to be paid before I begin," the barber said, "for although you look a gentleman, Señor, you might be something else."

"Well spoken!" the poet marveled beneath the tree. "I am writing everything down."

"You will be paid," said Fantasma, "if only you will rid me of the itch that has plagued me ever since I slept in a sacred place, and banish a saint's banter from a brain sorely craving entertainment."

The barber wrapped Fantasma's face in a steaming towel and prepared a generous amount of lavender-scented lather. Looking up, Phosphor marveled at all the wonderful little apparatuses installed in the tree: a small dung-fueled stove for the heating of water, a towel rack, a shelf for jars, another for brushes, scissors, and combs. Hoops of brass held bottles of soap and hair oil with French names: *L'abbé Fiard, L'arc en Ciel, La Verité Universelle.* Soon Fantasma's face vanished in suds, and Phosphor, delighting in the cloudless sky and limpid atmosphere, took out his tripod and his black box and seized the barber, the fantastic tree, and a soapy Fantasma riding a branch—forever.

"Many, many years ago," the barber began, "the coastal regions of Birdland teemed with an oversize clam-digging bird named—"

"The lôplôp!" Phosphor scribbled madly.

"When I was a young man," the barber continued as Fantasma's head cooked in its towel, "I decided—and my decision was precipitated by vanity—to hunt the coast until

I might find a tribe of those creatures that, by the time I was full grown, had become exceedingly rare. I had been told by a Moorish sailor that his queen was partial to rare things and had devoted an entire palace to the dead bodies of precious animals. I stalked the coast for many seasons, but the birds—being reasonable—had come to fear mankind and kept to themselves, never walking about except by night. At last, after months of searching, I saw a family sitting together on the rocks. They were facing out to sea and had their backs to me; so still were they that had not one of them begun to sing, I should have missed them. But moved by the beautiful moon and the mournful sound of the waves, and perhaps in remembrance of those distant days when the lôplôps were rulers of the island, long before any one of them had been made into a blanket, its great beak torn from its head to be used as a dish, the lôplôp lifted its face and sang a song that did little to move me. Thinking only of the excellent price its pelt would bring, I crept behind a rock and with my musket fired into the lot of them and watched as they fell with a thunderous thud; listened as they wept, bleeding to death on the sand.

"I approached to see the havoc I had done firsthand when a curiously melodious entreaty poured forth from the impressive beak of a bird I had wounded, but not mortally. It knelt before me in the most human way imaginable, and as its fellows gasped for air, the last lôplôp begged for its life. Deeply impressed, I wondered that a feathered monster should touch my heart. I recalled those stories continuing to circulate among us: how the aborigines refused to eat the lôplôp's flesh because, they said, 'The lôplôp begs for mercy like a man.'

"The more I listened, the more repentant did I become,

suffering an acute spiritual subtraction and regretting my evil deed. Listening to that bird's dirge, I realized the gravity of my act. The creature on its knees was the last of its line. But at that moment was produced a miracle: the creature, so like an animated wig, appeared to vacillate, to evaporate, to radiate! The beak vanished and in its place I saw a woman's face, her flowing hair, and then her body—slender and gracious and draped in sky blue veils. I recognized the Holy Mother and, falling at her feet, begged forgiveness. I promised her that should the creature I had harmed survive, I would thereafter care for it; that I should revere it as my educator; that as penance I should become that most ridiculous thing—a barber, and in a secluded place where I could spend the greater part of my time in prayer and devote myself to the well-being of the innocent creature I had impoverished irretrievably. Then, as the vision dissipated, the lôplôp sang again and I, first digging in the sand with my musket for a clam to offer it, after threw the weapon in the sea. Then, stalking up from the water's edge I reached this meadow and this tree. It glowed in the moonlight and it seemed like the Holy Mother was sitting in a barber chair on the branch where you sit. Thus I installed myself, and each day I walk down to the coast to converse with the last lôplôp (for I have mastered the creature's tongue), to brush its coat and polish its beak, to pray beside it (for I have taught it to pray) and to meditate upon the evil of the world."

Throughout this speech the barber had busied himself with Fantasma's head, so that once the tale was over, it appeared to solidify like a planet in gas. Phosphor, perceiving this, wondered if there were not a poetry of soap and hot water, and taking note that *soap* rhymes with *hope*, saw how hopeful Fantasma looked, how *new*—as if he had just been born.

"This is a holy tree," the barber continued, "by the pope's testicles I vouch for its sacred character, and by these many votive gifts you may see hanging from its branches. Once a cripple hobbled all the way from Pope Publius on crutches, only to jig all the way home again; and these are his crutches, hanging beside the braids of a maiden who, cured of vanity, bade me cut them off at the root, as she desired to enter the Order of Rosy Water upon her return to the city."

Just then Yahoo Clay appeared carrying a wildly gesticulating lobster in each hand; the pockets of his breeches bulged with shellfish. Little Pulco walked behind him with a pail of sea urchins hanging from the crook of his elbow and juggling with two hands a stupendous sole so heavy he could barely manage to carry it. Soon thereafter, Fogginius stumbled forth with several coconut cabbages, and within the hour the party was feasting beneath the tree, "the largest," Fogginius informed them, "in the world. For whilst the thug scaled the fish and gutted it, and dropped the lobsters in bouillon, I measured the trunk on my knees. Here," he continued, "we have at hand multiple examples of the visage of God: the tree, graceful and munificent; the cabbages, things peculiar-looking beyond belief and yet, when dressed, making for a king's salad; and the sole, a thing unshapely, weird, ludicrous, flat as a pancake with one blind, one beetling eye—and yet, how well-suited to our appetites! Sweet, flavorful, and firm!" As the saint spoke with his mouth full, the others took care to sit as far away from him as possible.

"Words have antiseptic properties," Fogginius belched, well pleased with his meal; "words are a puissant purge. See Yahoo Clay there," he pointed him out to the barber; "the wretch appeared to me in a climax of moral and physical feebleness that, prodded by impulsiveness, he had inflicted upon his own fickle person. I saved him with simples and cured him with conversation. With prodigiously clever arguments, I convinced him to abandon all lusts and instabilities, and when he pretended to sleep I prodded him and cried: 'Just as words are fixed to the air and sponges to the floor of the sea, so the human brain is fixed to words, and words shall prove your cure.' Is it not so, Clay? Tell the Druid" (for this is what he thought the barber to be) "how I talked you back to life!"

But all the while Fogginius spoke, Yahoo Clay had inched away, and having found a comfortable branch was sprawled on the verge of sleep. The others, too, had vanished, so that Fogginius, finding himself alone, was left to wonder upon mutabilities and at the transience of all things, including picnics. Having no one to talk to, he soon grew sleepy. Tumbling to the ground, he rolled himself up in his cloak and, tucked between two roots, he snored.

Sometime deep in the night, Phosphor awoke from a beautiful dream: he had returned to Pope Publius alone, not on a mule but a sprightly dappled horse, its mane threaded with silver bells. The sound of the bells filled the air as the poet entered the central plaza; everywhere he saw paper flags and festive banners and tables set with cakes and flasks of wine. Hearing a familiar voice call his name, Phosphor looked up and saw Professor Tardanza, merry and smiling, wave to him from a festooned balcony.

Suddenly Professor Tardanza's daughter was trotting beside him; together they rode to the marble steps of the cathedral. As Professor Tardanza's daughter was dressed from head to foot in a profusion of white lace, Phosphor knew this was their wedding day. They halted, and the poet leapt from his steed, lightly, hovering for a moment in the air above the ground, so that the throng that had followed them applauded. Taking his bride into his arms, Phosphor floated into the cathedral where the priest, who was Professor Tardanza, waited for them wearing a wig of butterflies. With surprise, Phosphor saw that everyone in the cathedral looked like Professor Tardanza: men, women, and children all had his face. Expressing his confusion to his bride, she laughed and said, "Yes! And look! They are all reading your book!" He saw then that each held a small volume of verse and muttered, "The volume is *very* slim!" "Ah," she replied, "only because each contains but one *stanza*." Her laughter filled his ears. "Have you forgotten? Your poem is far too long to fit into one volume! A library is under construction to house it; already it is the largest edifice in Birdland—look!" He turned and out the door could see, rising in the distance, a tower of many colors reaching for the sky. And as he looked, bursting with joy and pride, Professor Tardanza's daughter threw back her lovely head and began to sing the epithalamium Professor Tardanza had written to celebrate his daughter's marriage to the prestigious inventor and poet—to celebrate their love, the epic poem, the tower that (as they looked on) was thickening and rising higher and higher as though it would pierce the eye of God. The dreamer's blood was racing; Phosphor awakened with a pounding heart, the sound of his beloved's voice filling his ears; awoke to that voice—and it was amazing: he could still hear its sweetness palpable on the air.

An outsize yellow moon illuminated the sky. It looked like a barber's basin of hammered gold, and the poet, trembling with something akin to awe, slipped from his hammock, pulled on his boots, and, half naked, set off to discover the origin of that glorious sound washing across the thorny meadow, coming from the sea. His heart raced; he recalled the silver-tongued songs of the sirens and their dangers, but he could not stop himself. *Love*, he thought with feeling, *is nearly always fatal.*

The tenant of a lunar world animated by desire, Phosphor flew to the distant rocks marking the shore. When he reached the first high boulder, panting with delight, the sweetness of that mysterious song muddled his senses and he stumbled and fell to his knees. Truly it was the most gorgeous, the most melic sound he had ever heard. He searched for words, for rhymes, and could find none. He could recall only shipwrecks caused by voices near coral reefs, how pilots, bewitched, navigated directly into the embrace of death. But then, as he made his way around a great black boulder of volcanic glass, the song twisted, knotted, became supplication; the unknown voice seemed to be pleading for something; the poet thought: *pleading for its life!* Leaping to the beach, Phosphor saw a struggle in the shallow water, saw Yahoo Clay doing battle with—but what in the name of merciful haven was it? A nightmare? A mare-headed woman dressed in fleece? A bird-woman! Prodigiously beaked! Yahoo Clay was battering the body of a fallen lôplôp with his club; the brute was clubbing the mythical beast to death; the last of the lôplôps was being mashed to a pulp! Through the hammering of his own blood in his brains the poet could hear the creature's skull crack and, beneath a second blow, shatter. He saw the sand soak up the lôplôp's blood.

Later, after day had broken, a weird thing occurred. As

Phosphor, Fantasma, and the barber dug a deep pit in which to bury the headless, naked body (the barber had kept its skin for sentimental reasons), Phosphor unearthed a massive stone head that had lain there for centuries, perhaps. It was the howling head of a woman, her scalp a thrashing web of snakes: it was a Birdlandian Medusa, its features aborigine and stark. She appeared to be sticking her tongue out at Phosphor—at least, that is how the poet saw her—and if the sight of the lôplôp's murder had submerged him in acute distress, this second vision of horror within the hour precipitated the poet headfirst into a deeper despondency than he had ever known. To make matters worse, Clay, whom Fantasma had violently thrashed for killing their host's charge, was holding his own bleeding head with his hands and bellowing his despair all along the beach. Phosphor feared the sound would drive him mad.

❦

The loss of the lôplôp's voice was for the poet a terrible loss. It coincided with the ruination of a dream, and convinced him that his love for Professor Tardanza's daughter was hopeless. And it was a terrible loss for the barber too, whose existence was now devoid of meaning.

"To care for the last lôplôp," he confided to Phosphor as they sat together on a slab of volcanic glass overlooking the foaming sea, "imbued my days with sacred purpose. Life, at best, is unstable and fantastic and, for those of my profession, singularly absurd."

"Come, come!" Phosphor attempted to cheer him.

"Hair is dead," the barber insisted. "I might as well trim the nails of parakeets, or polish the scales of fish. I scrape it off, I cut it off, I pluck it from the ears—and still it grows back."

"It is alive!" the poet said.

"Only at the roots, which, unlike those of lust, cannot be contained."

"Ah!" said the poet. "Lust. *Contained?*"

"In youth one must occupy the mind," the barber told him, "else lose it to love. Long ago when I was spurned by a wench I wanted, I holed myself up in my room and wrote a complete *History of Wiggery*. I came to dream that one day I would be the world's supplier of ecclesiastical wigs. I designed a magnificent papal wig—"

"And so it was!" Fogginius had discovered them; spiderlike he scaled a rock and panting cried: "Eve's apple was a *fig!*"

"I was telling the poet how I once designed a papal *wig!*" the barber shouted: "A PAPAL WIG!"

"Nor do I"—his bones popping, the saint embraced the barber warmly—"give a fig for papality!" And seeing that both the poet and the barber looked at him oddly, he explained: "They took away my church, you see, because I asked the one question they could not answer: *What are the moral advantages of kneeling before an image on a stick?* Dead meat on a stick! One might as well worship *shish kebabs!* For this they called me a 'contaminating power'! Chased me from a chapel I'd built of coral—pink and white! Replaced me with a spineless mollusk green as infancy!"

"Once," the barber attempted to ignore him, "I designed a pubigerous wig in the shape of the Tower of Babel. I sent it to the pope for his birthday. The idea was that coming and going, and without uttering a word, the pope would deliver a Holy Message!"

"And what might that have been?" the poet asked.

"That man's ambitions are inflated."

"Kind of you to ask!" Fogginius beamed. "No one else has. But, sad to say, I am not better and continue to suffer. Our servant, Yahoo Clay, cannot cook to save his life."

"I invented a wig," the barber continued, "to be put on in haste should an angel spontaneously appear. A wig in the shape of a dove to be slipped on the head in a wink!"

"On the brink? Did you say *on the brink?* Are things as bad as that?" Fogginius scolded: "Come now. The world's still in its infancy."

"This peruke," the barber continued, "felicitated inter-course between worlds. It contained an echo chamber so that God's deep silence might reverberate about the pope's skull to tone and temper his mind. This was a winter wig, to keep the cranium safe from chills. It protected the brains from atmosphere, and the sound of the rabble crouching and hacking in their yards."

"The *sound?*" the poet wondered.

"Ear flaps. Providing protection from wind and the hum of many voices filling the air."

"If you wish to," Fogginius said grandly, stroking his greasy head with both hands, "you may wash my hair. One should try anything once, and I know you are sad today. If it will cheer you, well then, have your way with me!" And, horribly, he winked.

"A crested wig so vast," the barber was wildly gesturing, "that it could contain a dwarf who, sitting on the pope's head and looking out the back through cunningly concealed windows, might warn of tyranny from behind."

"—And maybe trim the sides a little, too . . ." Fogginius agreed. "But not too much."

"I invented a villous wig"—the barber looked at the

saint's skull with misgiving—"scented with vanilla to fla-
vor a pontiff's mind with peace. A wig so gigantic that in a
crowded room God might at once recognize His primate.
A wig for summer containing a hollow filled with cool air;
a winter wig sustaining a perpetual compost to keep a cardinal's head warm as toast; an acoustical wig in which a bishop
might hear the whispers of his conscience and the aerial
orchestras of angels. A wig honeycombed with absences in
which to stock a priest's gospelings. A wig of nettles—"

"*Clearly* as many camels as needles!" Fogginius shouted.
"Does *that* answer your question?"

"I made wigs until a tax was levied on hair, false or true,
and I could no longer afford to ply my trade, although my
last attempts included poison ivy to be sold to the senile
and the insane."

"To what *purpose?*" asked the poet.

"To *quicken* them, you see. Lastly I created a garniture of
rose leaves for the privacy of the bath. A wig conserves and
secures character," the barber sighed, "and so it is a noble
thing."

"The day I am a published and celebrated poet," Phosphor
said to him, for he was deeply moved, "I will have you make
a wig for *me!*"

"A wig for a poet?" Dejected, the barber pondered awhile.
"What could it possibly look like?"

"Macaroni!" cried Fogginius. Both the poet and the barber wondered why.

18

Ved—I return to the museum archives (I now have a key to the attic!) again and again in my attempt to reconstruct my island's history. This effort consistently rewards me, sometimes in tantalizing scraps: a badly foxed letter, a fractured ocularscopic plate, an iron glove bearing the Fantasma crest, a codpiece of red silk—or with a major discovery such as the previous portrait of Nuño Alfa y Omega the poet. But the past two days I have been drawn irresistibly to the natural history wing and that tantalizing view of Birdland as Lilliput and *yet another wonder* in an adjoining room I overlooked last week: a Brobdingnagian medusa, a full fifteen feet tall! Made of resins, I suppose; fiberglass, perhaps? And *cellophane!* Reduced to the size of a smelt, one stands beside it paralyzed by the artist's audacity. In a froth of excitement I ran back down to town and raised our old friend Boris from the lethargy retirement has imposed upon him, to prod him up the hill; he claims the medusa is scientifically perfect down to the smallest detail—and you know how scrupulous he can be. What, I wonder, will this mysterious Polly, this protean Polly, come up with next? (It occurs to me that we are both *reconstructing* something in a time so eager to *deconstruct!* If I were not so damnably shy (ah yes, that incapacity of mine has not lessened over the years) I would introduce myself. But as you know, the only time I ever dared entertain thoughts of courtship was when I dreamed of Lise who at this very moment is in the kitchen with her mistress preparing *sfogliatine saporite* for the Edible Ark's Saturday night menu!)

🐚

Clay's mood, like his master's, appeared to worsen. Once the party had taken leave of the bereft barber, who did nothing to detain them, Clay trudged behind the rest, muttering to himself and holding his mule by the tail. He looked so dark, so umbrageous, that the others feared him and wished the battle on the beach had come out differently. But then, the lôplôps had been known as much for their incapacity to protect themselves from harm as for their beautiful voices. One blow of that great beak could have shattered Clay's skull; instead, the creature had continued to sing, *as if a voice could still ferocity!* Phosphor wondered: *Could a voice inspirit the world? Embellish it and change it for the better?* Privately he feared that all poets would one day go the way of the lôplôp. *We are all birdmen,* he shuddered, *doomed.* As he and his mule passed beneath a tree so weighted down with parrots it creaked, he longed for exquisiteness, for beauty and peace.

The poet's nostrils quivered; the air was swimming with the fragrance of flowers, of wild honey and ripening fruit. Breathing deeply he thought it did not matter if his own voice was never heard, as long as Beauty continued to inspirit the world. Unjustly, it was at this precise instant of sweetness that Phosphor was cruelly struck upon the head and with such violence he tumbled from his saddle to the ground and rolled into a ditch. The missile—a spiny breadfruit—had been fired by Yahoo Clay from the treetop. Fantasma's mule gobbled and rearing, groaned; it nearly threw Fantasma. It too had been struck. For what seemed like an eternity, the entire party was bombarded.

"A stinkpot!" Fogginius could be heard hollering throughout that deadly weather. "A fumigation! A holy war!" And Clay was bellowing—that his brain was boiling, boiling so fast his head could not contain it . . . this brain was a pig roasting in the pit of his skull—

"Roasting in its own juices!"

"Silence!" Fantasma stood in his stirrups. "Not another word! Else I blow apart your mouth!"

"My brain's a soup of shit!" Clay pleaded from his perch. "Master! Climb up here and put your nose to my ear! You'll smell dung!"

Sometimes, the saint pondered to himself, *the cure is the malady.* "Thinking *stinks!*" Clay wagged his head this way and that as though attempting to unscrew it from the rest. "A call for stilts, master, to carry me across the sewer of my mind!"

"A call for quarantine!" Fogginius offered, attempting to get off the hook. "A quarantine and a curfew! The citizen has been bewitched! Bewitched by female sorcery!"

Pale as a ghost, Fantasma reached for his musket. *It's all over,* little Pulco thought. *I am dead and gone to hell.*

"My brain's ejaculating!" Clay was sobbing, "into God's fist!" Phosphor held his hands over his ears and in a fetal crouch groaned in his ditch for the mother he never had.

"I dream of fires!" Clay ranted, "and unlawful things! My way—ask Fogginius!—is marked by a turd. The way is marked by shit and leads to a pit of bones! So say ancient ge-, ancient ge-, geographer students of sharp edges, Fogginius told me their names: Christopher breaking like glass carbuncles, Christopher Carbuncle, *Karfunkel,* 'fenkelh' means, means—what in the name of Christ does it mean? 'To sparkle'! Ask Fogginius! Ask Fogginius! Ah! If I could count I could tell you how many seconds, minutes, hours, days, and weeks I spent crushed beneath the weight of his tutelage and how long each one was and how long each one lasted and how long—"

"Come down from there *now!*" Fantasma cried, pointing his gun, the red crest of his hair igniting the wood like a bonfire, "else I halve you in two!"

Halve him in two? pondered Phosphor. *Halve him in two?* But Clay was captive of his addled wits and could not stop. In an altered voice, and in a manner they recognized as belonging to Fogginius, he continued:

"Ah! Agony. Ah! Affliction. Ah! Alas. Ah—"

"ARCHITECTURE!" Fogginius approved. He could not stop himself.

"What is architecture?" Clay droned, "if it is not the brainchild of alphabet? the burial ground of animality? the alpha of exile from Eden? A tangible mathematics encrusted with the . . . the lime of, the lime of human pretension?"

It was then that a detonation pierced their ears—a sound so fierce the reverberating wilderness stilled to silence and they saw the thug's body caroming through branches and leaves, branches and leaves . . . and Clay lay dead at Phosphor's feet, the top of his skull torn off. Already the wound was black with flies.

Phosphor closed his eyes, knowing that hideous and disgusting details have a way of sticking in the mind. When he opened them, Pulco was pressing against him for comfort. A turtle had joined them in the ditch and although its head remained hidden, it clearly grieved and kicked with its four leathery feet. Fantasma, his musket smoking, stood over his strongman's corpse:

"If I hear the sound of another human voice," he said, "if anyone dares speak, *I will blow out his brains too.*"

They traveled towards evening in silence. Camp was made beside Galatea Bay's molluscan monument—that heap of dead shell we once mapped together, dearest Ved, proving the aborigines were shell-gatherers and that prior to the colonial invasion had inhabited the island for many thousands of years.

Clay gone, the party was forced to forage for itself, setting to work in the shallow coastal waters much as sea lions, knocking limpets from rocks with stones and digging for clams in the wet sand. The turtle, although simmered over a slow fire for six hours, proved too tough to eat. Had he dared speak, Fogginius would have informed them that terror had rendered it inedible.

That night, as Phosphor lay in his hammock unable to sleep, the sky appeared to part like a vast velvet curtain, revealing a sudden moon: a mask of gold and a pulsing heart, an inscrutable face, or a fist holding something very tightly; yes, the moon throbbed and trembled in the air, trembled with rage or desire, he could not say; it hung there in its ink like a lantern or a golden pear fallen from the table of the gods; it pulsed like those sexual shellfish—*Modiolus vagina*—the poet had (the blood rushing to his ears) devoured for his supper.

In haste, Phosphor inked a "moonish list" to be used

later, although he feared the moon's capacity to fill his brain with images might subvert his own intention in the end. Giddy, he scribbled: *I cover these pages with ink yet have no inkling why.* And then, before he could stop himself, before he realized what he was doing, he found himself writing a letter to Professor Tardanza:

Honored Professor:

Animated by the moon in a forest so thick with parrots the ground is incandescent with feathers, I balance in my hammock, the near sea thundering, wide awake despite the ardors of the day, for my heart is not mine but another's, its seizures aggravated by distance. And yet I am contented, too, because the air I breathe is the air she breathes; we breathe the same particles of air, and we sleep, or do not sleep, beneath the same luminous eye that tonight is an adoring eye, weeping. Even now, you see, I dream, I dream of her. I dream—he repeated—*of her.*

Then, in a fever and firm in his resolve, Phosphor leapt to the ground and prodding Pulco in the ribs, woke him.

"You must," said the poet, "you *will* take this missive to Pope Publius, take your mule and go now, beneath the moon, and once you are there, give this to Professor Tardanza himself, *no other.* For I have had a revelation and it is this: Life is but a rent in the wing of a moth and love an unquenchable fire, and I must marry her else die."

"Nuño Alfa y Omega!" little Pulco cried out in childish terror, hopping about like a wounded bird—for Clay's murder had rattled him irretrievably—"Don't die! Don't die!" He threw his arms around the poet, his guardian and master—and the only member of the party who treated him with disinterest. The sight of Clay's swarming wound had deeply distressed him; he saw Death's gaping maw every-where, even in the charred shells scattered about their cold fire.

"My life is in your hands," the poet said. "You must leave at once. Take this letter; do not lose it or soil it."

At first sight of the morning star and in the heavy dew of the early hours, little Pulco set off.

"Her hair is as heavy, as fragrant, as pollen," Phosphor called out after him. "Tell her I said that."

19

When morning came, Fantasma was enraged: Pulco was useful to them all. Henceforth, Phosphor had to perform all menial tasks—such as preparing the breakfast gruel and helping his hated stepfather off and on and on and off his mule, in and out his hammock, and out and in his boots, as well as with the least gratifying details of his toilet.

Fogginius, having forgotten Fantasma's threat of the previous day and even Clay's violent end—and, for that matter, everything that had happened recently—and believing himself to be on an important papal mission, unsure, even, of his own identity, was, with a growing certitude cemented by disparate signs visible only to himself, tottering at the edge of Ultimate Illumination: that he, Fogginius, *was* pope. He began to yammer, as if all life and muscle were contained in his jaws.

The rest of him was visibly waning; he could not reach for his own elbow without decrepitating—a brittle *pop* like the sound of distant musket fire, a fusillade of crackles and reports so loud that, had the saint not been already deaf, these could have deafened him, surely.

"The boy's been seized by cannibals!" Fogginius cried out,

spitting porridge unintentionally into the poet's face—for he was suddenly aware that the little buttocks he so liked to pinch were nowhere near. "Who will wipe a pontiff's arse and pass him his plate?"

Phosphor audibly groaned, knowing all too well the answer. But he suffered for love; he humbled himself for love!

"Pulco is on an urgent errand," the poet explained, "and we will wait here for his return."

"I have decided," said Fantasma, "that I shall explore the coast alone—that stretch of sand we see from here, and the rocky ridge. I hope to catch a glimpse of a mermaid. I would so like to fuck a mermaid." He scratched his balls and continued dreamily: "It must all be contained within the ocularscopic box: the sea, the waves, those grottoes yonder, like wounds in the underbelly of the world. I want it all—can it be done? The very quality of the air." He was feeling powerful again, and greedy. He pointed to the places he would have Phosphor capture on glass once Fogginius' needs had been met with for the day.

"Well and good!" (click!) Fogginius cried. "Wander where you will! I have much to share with my friend the bishop" (clack! clock! tock!). The saint stabbed the poet's heart affectionately.

Phosphor scowled. He was exhausted, tired of the open air, of carting camera and chemicals across the roots and rubble of the world. His thoughts had not been his own for days—had it been weeks? He was Fantasma's thing, an appendage to his hallucination.

"Snakes!" Fantasma cried out. "I should like to have them coupling in the grass. All manner of copulations—the entire animal kingdom. An historic collection. The private lives of pythons, parrots, primates, porcupines, and pigs. And then, once we are home again, the fornications of the citizenry in its entirety. Peasants on couches of mud, brides deflowered in rooms smelling of lavender." He moaned. "You must seize the private parts of every living creature on the island."

"Meringues!" Fogginius was speaking to himself. "One half-pound. . . ." A string of drool dropped from his lips and webbed its way down his grizzled chin.

"Corpses, Nuño . . ." Fantasma mused. "We'll take your black box to the morgue. Last night I dreamed a head was growing from the center of my face," he recalled, turning pale. "It has just come back to me. A hideous head—hairy and hungry. A famished head, gnashing its teeth. I begged it to leave me in peace. But it was voracity itself and devoured everything in its path—boulders, anthills, cows, windmills . . . and I was forced to follow helplessly behind. Ruled by it! Utterly ruled! And *ruined*. Ruined and ruled!"

"The nightmare," Fogginius whispered, his voice fractured and thin, "is a cold wind raging within the mind. The nightmare is an amalgam. It contains:

    The sulphur of ingested rage
    The feces of fear
    The resin of unrequited love
    The urine of ingested falsehoods
    The owls of unresolved quarrels
    The jackals of jealousy
    The knots and snot of perplexity. . . ."

But Fantasma did not hear this list, for he had wandered off, clutching his face and cursing.

Looking infinitely dejected, Nuño Alfa y Omega attempted to feed Fogginius his gruel. *My life*, he thought, *has come full circle. I am not my own master.* So dark were Phosphor's thoughts that a small cloud appeared to orbit his head—although it might have been a silent swarm of flies. (The three men sorely needed to bathe.)

I am a mere thing of Fantasma's fantasy, Phosphor thought. *To hell with the ocularscope! At home in my impoverished rooms, who knows what I might have dreamed up by now. For such a thing as moving pictures glimmers deep in my brain, flickers, dies, flames anew. . . . A thing, I think, not impossible.*

Just then Fantasma's mule kicked and brayed, possessed, or so it seemed. Burdened with the graceless task of bringing it to its senses, Fantasma hollered for Phosphor. The dream of images in a continuum vanished from the poet's mind.

"I shall mend my mind with exercise and pleasure," Fantasma told Phosphor. "Wait for me. I won't be gone but a day or two."

After breakfast, the poet settled Fogginius, visibly waning, in the cool shade of a fern as furred as a spider, and gave himself over to thoughts of Professor Tardanza's daughter. Once when Fogginius, waking, began pontificating—DO STARS CAUSE EVIL?—the poet, his ears insufficiently plugged with beeswax, audibly sighed.

"You are in love!" the saint wagged a finger. "Better I remain silent."

The days passed; Fantasma did not return. Phosphor succumbed to revery. If Fogginius had not raked him from his fantasies by calling out from time to time *gooseberry fool!* and *milk candy!*, Phosphor would have forgotten to eat. Suddenly ravenous, on uncertain feet, he would totter off to gather irregularia and oysters; once, he managed to capture a crab. But Fogginius, now so thin as to appear made of parchment, refused all nourishment—although he continued to carry on like a child in a bakery.

One afternoon he called Phosphor to his side.

"You do not know this," he said, "no one does. But once I had a son. . . ." He attempted to rise; the forest responded with the retorts of his shattering bones and snapping tendons. Startled, Phosphor looked on as the saint disarticulated before his eyes and collapsed with a sigh into a heap of knucklebones and pale ashes. Even his skull imploded, like the thin shell of an egg on the fire. Fogginius' jaws, which for several instants appeared to work the air, also turned to dust. It was then that the poet realized the extent of the old man's sorcery: evidently an act of superlative necromantic will had held those enfeebled parts together long after their time had run out.

My God! Phosphor wondered, *I have been harboring, humoring a cadaver. Perhaps,* he considered later, enjoying his solitude deeply, *perhaps his listeners were the glue that kept him fused. Perhaps . . .* he mused further, *language is the glue that held my stepfather together.*

He began another scrap of verse, this time to no one in particular, but to:

> *My fellow man who must needs find*
> *Meaning and Purpose, else lose Hope and Mind.*

And then, in response to Fogginius' definition of nightmare, he proposed this portrait of the dream: *She is an airy tincture of a fragrant rain, the brightest flowers, all the colors of China and Persia combined, the mystery of weather and shells breathing beneath the sea.*

20

On the second day, Pulco, who had not slept the night before, fearing the speaking serpents and silent dogs and scarlet flowers shaped like human hands Fogginius had once evoked in order to instruct him, came upon a barren stretch of land staggered with mounds and littered with rubble. His mule advanced tentatively, as though wading through eggs, and Pulco was submerged by the uncanny conviction that a rock was looking at him. To conjure his terror, he spoke out loud: *Tricks of light and shadow*, recalling how Phosphor had once demonstrated how the eye can deceive the mind. Phosphor had penned little images for Pulco: of a vanishing amphora made of two faces in profile; anamorphic skulls and ships, and, once, naked figures embracing. Little Pulco had, at once, copied these, demonstrating to the surprise of both that his own hand was surer than his master's. But now the rock continued to fix him with its one venomous eye, and as the boy progressed across that haunted swath stretching before him like a ruined city, another eye appeared from yet another lump. At that instant the moon tore free from the clouds that had held it fast, and Pulco looked on transfixed with terror as the entire landscape crumbled and reassembled into animated life. Everywhere eyes, feet, and fists generated spontaneously. A mysterious face winked at him from the summit of a fissured boulder, and a phallus pointing skyward designated a fiery red triangle: flamingos winging their way to sea. For the first time in his young life it occurred to Pulco that there were other islands—for the birds atomized above the horizon and all that evening did not reappear.

Fixing the distance into which the birds had vanished, Pulco was soon embraced by the familiar and extravagant vegetation. And that night as he fell asleep pressed to the mule's hot body, he said out loud, to test the possibility: *There are other islands.*

Late the following day, as the sea was set on fire along the western rim, Pulco saw a sinister commotion in the air: a wheel of vultures orbited the masts of a gutted ship seized by coastal rocks. The wreck vomited a stench so acute the mule, usually docile, began to scream. Pulco recognized the slave galley belonging to Señor Fantasma. As soon as he was able, he got down from his mule and defecated into the greater eye of an anthill to exorcise the smell of death lingering near him.

That evening, Pulco entered Pope Publius. Famished, weary, and sad, he and his mule made their way to Professor Tardanza's gate. Wonderful aromas flooded the courtyard and as Pulco reached the servant's entrance his knees shook. For many long minutes he hammered the door impatiently with his filthy fists until the ivy-covered wall beside him swung open on rusty hinges and the cook appeared, wielding a spoon the size of an oar.

"A letter!" Pulco shouted, leaping back and using it to shield his face. "From the poet, Nuño Alfa y Omega!" He peered out from behind the letter and saw that the cook had not raised her spoon against him but was, instead, leaning on it. "To Professor Tardanza," he repeated. Shyly, he smiled.

To his delight, Pulco was both relieved of the letter and invited into the kitchen where the servants were eating together: the cook, the housemaid, an itinerant laundress, and the cook's sister-in-law. The delectable smells proved misleading, for all were eating porridge and, indeed, Pulco's bowl was no better. Seeing his disappointment, the cook explained that this was a porridge of Professor Tardanza's invention made of four different grains, including birdseed, and that if it did not taste very good, it was sure to make him immortal. If the professor and his family had dined on roasted birds, roasted peppers, roasted corn on the cob, and fried bananas, it was only because they needed to raise the temperatures of their brains prior to sleeping: the professor hoped to investigate his family's dreams. So far his attempts had proved fruitless: *none* of the Tardanzas dreamed. The cook informed Pulco that she dreamed incessantly, as did her sister-in-law. Their dreams were far too humble to interest Professor Tardanza, although on Thursday the cook had dreamed of a treasure of golden eggs and the map that led to it.

For dessert they shared a steamed pudding of fourteen different sorts of husks. After supper Pulco was given a bath in a great copper cauldron. As the housemaid and the cook's sister-in-law looked the other way, the cook—far too ugly to cause any embarrassment—scrubbed Pulco free of grit, lice, scabs, and fleas.

"Poor child!" she cried as she soaped his head for the third time. "Your masters are barbarians!"

She also washed his clothes, dried them before the fire, and mended them. Once the boy was presentable, she sent him to an antechamber where a number of Professor Tardanza's students were waiting.

Because he was shy, Pulco turned his gaze to the ceiling, which opened out to an oval expanse of pale blue sky— although he knew it was near midnight and could not be morning. The blue oval was orbited by angels; their plump buttocks hung suspended overhead like ripening peaches. Turning his eyes to the wall, he saw a niche just large enough to contain one brimming glass of amber-colored wine, a handful of cherries, and a cookie spangled with sugar. Reaching out, Pulco's hand hit the wall; the niche, just as the ceiling, was a beautifully painted illusion. As he passed his hand across the smooth surface, his heart fluttered madly.

"Don't be fooled by the bag of money hanging in the water closet," one of the students addressed him. "The peg it hangs from is equally fake."

Weak with amazement, Pulco sat gaping in his chair. Sometimes he stared at the ceiling, sometimes at the niche. Soon the students' voices disturbed his thoughts and he found himself listening to them intently. Their conversation was incomprehensible, although Pulco was later able to reconstruct it in part for Phosphor. For example, he would recall the subjects of several animated arguments: whether or not gravity exists in Paradise; if, in the hands of the Creator, air is malleable; if the brain ceases to function in deep sleep and which organ produces dreams: the liver, the heart, the brain, or the eye. They also discussed at length, and in hushed voices, an experiment that had recently been performed by Professor Tardanza: he had managed to capture the nightmare of an insane woman by means of a glass melon bell held in place above her head. A vapor had collected within the bell and was precipitated into a cruet. Heated gently for seven days, the nightmare coagulated and turned the color of strong tea. Having received a drop of this infusion in their water dish, twelve parakeets died.

Another student had brought along a list of objects he had dreamed over the past six months, as well as the frequency with which he had dreamed them:

nests: 64

bushes: 40

thistles: 75

brambles: 9

cuttlefish: 2

sea urchins: 20

epidemics: 9

clothes brushes: 89

fur: 1

rabid dogs: 1

As the students began a long discussion on the manner in which the Great Flood had transformed the original configuration of the world, and little Pulco, his belly full of macerating grains and husks, was nodding off to sleep, the housemaid called him to come forth and to meet, at last, Professor Tardanza.

The walls of Professor Tardanza's study were burning with maps of those islands the boy had intuited but, because he was unschooled, could not see; a geographical alphabet he could not read. These maps caused the walls to splinter into elements his active imagination put form to: here a boot, there a bull's head, a donkey, a slab of cheese. He saw an open book, a hook, an overturned vase of flowers. His own island, shaped like a green egg, hung behind Professor Tardanza, who was standing and whose beard was so shiny and pointed it looked sharp enough to slice meat. His eyes, too, were intensely piercing, and Pulco thought they could see through his flesh to his very bones. He protected his thrashing heart with his hand and looked down at his own impeccable feet with surprise.

"Name?" Professor Tardanza's voice was unaccountably shrill. The boy hesitated. His name circled the room twice, hitting the walls and ceilings with its wings before perching once again in Pulco's mind.

"Pulco."

"Are you *certain?*" Pulco's name tumbled from its perch. He attempted to speak and found he could not. Professor Tardanza was now standing very close to Pulco. His hair, his clothes smelled of gravy and caramel.

"Profession?"

Two large tears spilled from Pulco's eyes.

"Courier!" Professor Tardanza answered for him. "It means you deliver letters! Letters of consequence, even! Philosophical letters! Missives of love! *Do you know how to read?*"

Pulco shook his head sadly. Tears fell from his face to his feet. He watched them dissolve between his big and little toes.

"Furthermore, you deliver them on blind faith! You deliver them *unread*. How do you know," and he rattled the poet's parchment in Pulco's face, "that it is not here written: *Take this boy, tie him to a post, and thrash him till he's purple?*"

Pulco gasped.

"This letter," Tardanza continued, "could very well say:

Roast this boy in a very slow oven and feed him to the archbish-op's pigs! This letter," slowly, methodically, he began to crush it in his fist, "is rubbish. But no matter. We will give the dreamer what he wants, and we will hope he gets nothing less than what he deserves." Grabbing Pulco by the ear, he pulled him from the room. "You will take with you what you are about to see," Tardanza continued, "and deliver it to Nuño Alfa y Omega the poet. You are a bright boy—yes! Yes! I can tell by the depth of your eyes. Terrified, unedu-cated, but intelligent." Taking up an oil lamp, he nudged Pulco down a corridor painted to look like a forest full of parrots. Turning a corner, they came to a room flooded with candlelight. At the threshold, Pulco rubbed his eyes with disbelief, for there upon a white counterpane, blushing, yet seemingly asleep, lay Professor Tardanza's daughter. She was entirely naked. Pulco knew that she was real because she breathed, and because her body gave off a scent of freshly sliced apples. Little Pulco, only nine, felt the milk teeth of first desire nibble at his tender prick.

"Tell the poet that just as you see her here, my daughter, Extravaganza, is his." Somehow Professor Tardanza had shut the door and Pulco found himself staring at a knot in the wood the shape and size of his own open mouth. As they retraced their steps down the corridor, Pulco thought he discerned muffled laughter like little bells.

"She is beautiful," Tardanza sighed, "but like her mother and myself, she *cannot dream.* Is it true that your master, Nuño Alfa y Omega the cripple, *dreams?*"

"He . . ." Pulco gathered his wits together—no simple task, for like moths they were hurling their fragile selves against the burning glass of Tardanza's lamp. "He . . ." Pulco sputtered, floundered, and then began again, scowling with the effort. "He dreams of *her*. He dreams of her . . . *all the time*."

That night the child slept fitfully beside the kitchen hearth. He dreamed of pantries filled with fictive things to eat: turkey, oysters, moons of orange cheese. In the morning, having filled himself with guava paste and an entire pan of sweet rolls, it came to him that before taking his message to his master, he must quickly go to Fantasma's house for news of Cosima. But, vast as he knew the house was, sprawling and substantial, *it had vanished*. Its disappearance was impossible, uncanny. Pulco recognized a path's turning, a tree, a certain wall; he recognized the avenue of palms, the fabulous front gate of tortured iron, but beyond saw nothing—only a wasted space that, greening, became gardens, overgrown yet familiar, and further—Fantasma's abandoned bananas.

The riddle was so excessive that Pulco simply spurred his mule and set off the way he had come, taking care to avoid, by several leagues, the stinking galley. His passage was noted by Birdland's own Officer of the Inquisition, Rais Secundo, who, perched in a tree, was marveling at what he assumed to be a demonic intervention.

But Pulco could not circumvent that cataclysmic and lunar terrain where he had wandered, so full of terror, only days before. He reached it towards evening, when the shadows etched the land fantastically, and moving among them, fingered, as it were, by darkness and by light, he suddenly recognized the formless, transitory nature of the world; recognized for one fleeting and exceptional instant that he was himself a fragment, a shadow, and a seeming; that those tumbled geometries, so like the splintered alphabets of some gigantic fallen frieze, mirrored, somehow, his own bones, his own inarticulate thoughts.

The experience, as instantaneous as it was profound, left him shaken and thoughtful. From that moment, little Pulco had eyes with which to recognize that Fantasma's attempt to seize the mutable world was doomed. As if to punctuate this momentous discovery with an exclamation point of fire, the sky, until then milky, cracked at the seams an electrical red.

21

Ved—I can hear you rumble: "This has gone too far! Must truth yield to *magick?* Up till now the work was fanciful but not—as I had been assured from the start—a work of *fancy*. An entire house does not vanish in the air except in fairy tales. What justifies such frivolity?"

Patience! I shall now take up Cosima's story there where I left off, and demonstrate how such a thing is possible, after all.

The pirate prince, who, as you will recall, had set up commerce on the beach, enravished Cosima the moment she set eyes on him. He wore his balls in a codpiece of red silk, and his pistols in a diamond-studded sling across his heart. His body was burned the color of mahogany, his nostrils flared, his teeth were excellent, and his one eye capable of igniting dead stars. In exchange for a ruby choker, Cosima was more than willing to give him a kiss. She called the necklace cheap, not dear enough—and wondered aloud if it was not worth much, much more. Teased beyond endurance, the pirate lifted her up in his huge arms and in the questionable privacy of his tent—its floor littered with marrow bones, gold dust, and stolen carpets—raised her skirts with his prick and extracted the jewel's true worth. Yet, by day's end, Cosima insisted she had not paid dearly enough; in fact, her debt increased, swelled with every passing hour.

At week's end the pirate's plunder had moved from the beach and into the parlors of Pope Publius. He was ready to set sail and made his way to Cosima's balcony, where she napped dreaming of him and dressed only in the shadows of flamboyants and a mane of hair. There he insisted she join him.*

Cosima agreed on one condition: *that they bring her house along*—for, she nibbled his nipples, she was *so* fond of it. That night, and the next and the next, for many ensuing nights, one hundred and one pirates carried off Fantasma's ancestral house stone by stone. They took everything:** costly niched statues from all the corridors, leaving the niches empty; took the niches next, the corridors after. But because they were not masons but sailors, they neglected to number the stones. Fantasma's house could not be rebuilt once the lovers reached Cuba.

---

* I have reason to believe Cosima's pirate is the mysterious author of *Voyages around the Known Universe* who was burned in Havana for claiming the world orbited the sun.

** They also took the cook and the housemaid and, needless to say, pillaged the wine cellar.

22

After a long journey back to the place where Pulco had left the poet, he found him hanging by his ankles from a guanabana tree. Once Pulco had managed to liberate him and Phosphor had regained consciousness, the poet explained that he had thus strung himself up because he expected the increased pressure of blood on the brain to intensify his imaginative capacities. Because he could not offer Professor Tardanza's daughter real orchids—being so far away—he had attempted in this manner to offer her the orchids of his longing. But within minutes he had passed out and he had no idea how long he had been hanging upside down. As his clothes were badly soiled with bird droppings and a lizard had taken up residency in the leg of his breeches, the poet supposed he had not been conscious for three days at least. He was very thin and his beard had grown upwards towards his ears. It seemed to Pulco that the poet's face was longer than ever and supposed his sojourn in the air had somehow stretched it. I believe at that moment, Pulco may have had an intimation of gravity.[*]

---

[*] Pulco's own unique career is worthy of another book.

Despite exhaustion, Pulco bathed and shaved the poet, then cooked a rice gruel for them both. Restored, they sat together quietly at the fireside, and only then did the boy notice the small heap of bones and ashes a vole returned to tentatively again and again—all that remained of Fogginius the saint.

"That little gnarled bit is the root of his tongue," Phosphor told Pulco, pointing. "His brain and all the other organs have atomized." Pulco nodded. Such a thing could no longer surprise him.

"I saw a field of bones," he said to Phosphor; "a field of bones; a field of stones; a field of fire."

"I like that!" the poet said, looking at Pulco with aston- ishment. "May I put it in my poem? It would work well with a thought that came to me:

> "*Man is but a particle of soot in the eye of Time.*"

Pulco knew enough to nod appreciatively.

> "*Man is but a particle of soot in the eye of Time,*
> *A teardrop in the brine of Infinity.*

"Or it could be Eternity . . . Infinity, Eternity. Eternity, Infinity . . . or maybe: Eternal Acrimony.

> "*A drop in the bucket of Eternal Acrimony.*

"Or even *Infinite* Acrimony."

For a time Pulco listened as the poet fussed, wondering why he had not asked about Professor Tardanza's daughter. Had all that blood that had gone to his head addled his brain? At last he spoke up.

"Master," said Pulco, "your request has been granted. I have spoken to Professor Tardanza. I have seen his daughter."

The poet moaned. "Granted," he whispered. "Seen her."

"She was asleep," said Pulco. "And she was . . . undressed. She is ever so beautiful."

"Undressed!" Phosphor looked perplexed, but then he beamed. "How thoughtful of her father, come to think of it," he decided. "After all, now we know she has no unsightly moles. No extra nipples."

"She appeared to blush," said Pulco. "She was very pink." The boy, fiercely blushing now himself, whispered, "Master?"

"Yes?"

"There is one thing . . . she doesn't dream!"

"Doesn't dream!" Phosphor was ecstatic. "A woman who doesn't dream!"

At this moment Fantasma stumbled forth from the brambles and vines, studded with thorns, visibly bruised and enraged. He had lost his musket and his clothes were mostly gone.

"I have had enough!" he announced. "If I can little stomach the company of men, the forest is far worse. There really is nothing there I want. And if the coastal waters here are empty of sirens, they are thick with sharks. My ancestors subjugated this island," he reminded them, "and yet out there in the thick of things . . . all that . . . *generative functioning*, I feared at any moment I would be devoured and digested."* He stood now beside their little fire and they

---

* Says Ombos: *Throughout his travels, Gulliver devours with his eyes—the queen's mouth, the handmaidens's nipples, her vulva, the decapitated head, the cancerous breast, the outsized lice. By tale's end he is stuffed; incapable of taking any more in, he is incapacitated by the sight of other human beings—all guilty of copulation, if only by default. If the phallic eye kills and is rendered impotent by what it perceives (its fangs retract*

could see that he was covered with swellings.

"Bees," he explained, "the size of hummingbirds." Fantasma's head was smeared with something indescribable. "An egg." Gingerly he touched what was left of his hair with bloodied fingers. "Christianity is annulled here," he brooded. "'Tis a hellish place wherein an ape can hurl an egg at a man and go unpunished."

Phosphor listened intently. Rarely had he heard Fantasma say so much. This ranting delighted him; it meant Fantasma too was ready to return to the city. The next thing Fantasma said was:

"Let us return to Pope Publius. We shall devote ourselves to an Entire Itinerary of the Civilized World as Perceived by Fango Fantasma. We shall create a Theory and Practice of Order. We shall meditate upon Harmony in the shape of *my beautiful house*. Its gracious quadrangular rooms! *Why didn't I think of this sooner?*" he wondered aloud. "*Why did I inflict this detour in chaos upon myself?*" And he punched himself so soundly in the nose that Pulco and Phosphor heard the cartilage crack.

"My house!" Fantasma continued, sobbing, the gears of his mind moving faster than they ever had before, "is smack in the center of the visible universe. Fogginius—*Fogginius!*

---

at the sight of Medusa's teeming scalp; verily it is outnumbered a hundred to one!) the mouth is female and monstrous because it opens into the secrets of the hoary deep; it activates the body's reeking machinery. When the queen of Brobdingnag takes up at a mouthful as much as a dozen farmers could eat at a meal, she is revealing something terrible about female famishment and capacity for defilement; see Chloe shit:

Distortions, Groanings, Strainings, Heavings;

like Rabelais' Gargamelle's, her leavings are prodigious, her visceral activity seismic (and is she shitting or giving birth?). . . . The queen at table offers something else to think about: if the table separates the top half of her body from the bottom, Gulliver stands precisely upon this Great Divide. Above him the queen crams; beneath him she digests. No wonder the little cricket man, Grildrig, feels dizzy! He is suspended between two horrors: the queen's mouth and her Royal Bum!

Where the devil is he?—told me. It has a left side and a
right side and a roof that does not leak! It contains venerable
objects that *all have names*—unlike . . . unlike . . ." again
he appeared to crush some living thing to dust beneath his
boot, "this open sewer . . ." his nose was bleeding now, "this
cunt! Toothed and tusked!

"My house!" Fantasma was dying of nostalgia, "how I
miss its *measurable* rooms! We shall ascertain their length
and width and height. We shall number every nail and every
fork and spoon!" He thought silently for a moment, then
said: "The entire Fantasma estate cataloged for the sake of
history and harmony! Ah!" He noticed now that little Pulco
was asleep at Phosphor's feet. "The little messenger is back!"
He gave the boy a kick. "Rise up!" he barked, "and find
Fogginius. Pack the mules. Prepare breakfast. Polish my
boots. We are going home."

"Sir," Pulco pleaded, weeping with fatigue, "I have only
just returned from the city and am so sorely tired. And I
cannot wake the saint, for he is *dead*."

Phosphor looked at Pulco then, perhaps for the first time.
He saw how tired he was, how threadbare; that his feet were
bleeding, his ribs heaving, his eyes circled by dark rings.

"I too would rest," Phosphor said, "and you, Señor, must
bathe those bites and bandage your face and spend the night
in sleep. You are a good child," he then turned to Pulco;
"I am profoundly grateful. Vanity has blinded me, I see
that now, and passion too. He deserves to sleep," Phosphor
said to Fantasma, "and also to think. And—why not?—to
play. This little boy," he continued, gazing fondly upon little
Pulco, who was more bewildered than pleased and weeping with exhaustion, "has assured me the hand of Professor
Tardanza's daughter. I am to marry upon our return!"

Fantasma stood agitated and uncomprehending. "His *body!*" he cried. "What has become of the holy remains?"

"This is all that is left." Phosphor dropped the corrugated residue into Fantasma's hand. "Time and Mother Nature saw to the rest." Fantasma's expression was one of horror.

"It is a vestige of his tongue," Phosphor explained, "which never ceased to wag."

"A miracle!" Fantasma looked at the thing with awe. "I shall have a reliquary made for it. A reliquary and a chapel. God is great!" Fantasma marveled. "The proof is here." In the moonlight, the nugget gleamed convincingly.

Meanwhile, at this very instant, Rais Secundo, Insomniac, Grand Inquisitor, and Ecclesiastical Judge, is contemplating a curiosity that has come into his hands—it is not clear how: an ocularscopic slide of glass upon which Cosima, twinned, stands clad scantily, the soft sphere of a breast and the smooth sphere of a knee gleaming like planets in a mysterious light that can only be called supernatural. These illuminations bring nothing so much to mind as fruit; the child is sweeter than a handful of ripe figs.

So hot is this image of Cosima that the old investigator's vestments, lastingly damp, have dried to the brittleness of antique parchment. A dwarfed cactus abandoned between two bald walls suddenly decides to flower. The blossom is scarlet, fleshy, and strange.

His mind fizzing and popping like carbonated water, the Inquisitor bolts the door to his chamber in the tower, scatters a moat of holy salt around the base of his chair, and sits ready for sudden attack, knowing that despite all precautions, a demoness of Cosima's evident capacities may, straddling a broom, a straw, a fingerbone, the pistil of a flower, enter through his window as smoothly as a worm enters an apple.

Jangling with keys, Secundo—on fire, the little image winking in his lap—lifts his robes and, grabbing his purple member, as gnarled as a dry lump of ginger, ejaculates into the flames of a public execution, comes in rooms full of wizards wearing peaked caps, ejaculates into the mouth of a witch, into the cup of the Holy Grail; ejaculates into the wounds of the Christ, comes in the hair of witches, comes in rooms carpeted with the flayed skins of choirboys, comes beneath the bloated feet of a hanging man, is embraced by apes and green monkeys, ejaculates into the Pope's miter; ejaculates into the anus of the Pope.

23

At daybreak, encumbered by Phosphor's equipment, which seemed heavier than when they set out, as if images could add weight to glass, as if having set out with empty cases one returned with creatures full-fleshed and thick-boned, they traveled until the fall of night, when Fantasma suddenly reined in his mule and cried:

"*Married!* I have not given you leave! Your marriage, Nuño Alfa y Omega, does not fit into my plans."

"Love has grown a beak within my heart," Phosphor countered. "I must marry as soon as I can else be pecked to death. Were I to die, I could no longer serve you."

"Hark!" Fantasma cried, ignoring him. "Did you hear that?"

"I heard only the silence of my own thoughts," Phosphor replied, "a silence sweet beyond belief."

"I heard *Fogginius!*" Fantasma crowed, "speaking as plainly as if he were here beside me . . . more exactly, as if he were a gnat sitting in my ear and speaking directly into my brain." Both Pulco and Phosphor held their breaths, preferring not to know what Fogginius, now a ghost, if anything, had to say.

"He has warned me of female treachery and of the night's darkness and insists we stop now, else be knocked off our mules by arboreal snakes, crushed to death, and slowly digested. Let us descend to the shore at once and find ourselves a nice patch of beach."

They came in time to a small finger of land. Walking to its furthest point, Fantasma declared this was a place where one could sleep in peace—for its entire territory, save for a small natural bridge, was circumscribed by water.

"Every part of this promontory may be perceived by the naked eye." Fantasma, who never smiled, almost beamed. "One could map it in an hour. *The saint inspirits the path.*"

The peninsula, a mere thirty yards long, very flat, and of milky sand, was devoid of interest.

"We shall spend the night here," Fantasma said, "and shall sleep in the certitude that nothing will throw itself upon us from a tree."

"Your chosen bedchamber is illusory," Phosphor prophesied. "I prefer to sleep with little Pulco on higher ground, among the weeds."

"*All* is illusion," Fantasma pontificated. "Fogginius said it often enough. *We are but a company of spirits*, he said, *floating through Cosmical Mind.* But here—Pulco, go catch some crabs, for famishment is real enough!"

Later, in his dream, little Pulco, sick of soul, saw Fantasma's house disengage and, stone by stone, lift into the air. He saw the graceful arches of the balconies, where Cosme had once somersaulted, slithering skyward; saw the ornamental porches and the pantry's narrow steps lift into an absolutely cloudless sky. Saw the chandeliers spitting smoke and soaring heavenward like sheet lightning. And the kitchen pots, mops, casseroles, and cups; and studded chairs; and the carved chests filled with linens, and cabinets with clothes; and those dishes upon which could be seen all the known races of men standing proudly naked beneath baobabs, or crouching in igloos, or crossing expanses of sand on camel hump. And then the child saw a dish upon which he and the poet, Phosphor, had been painted: two forlorn figures moving through a tropical forest on mules about to be seized by gargantuan snakes grinning among the orchids:

There is a snake for you and a snake for me, the poet spoke to the child in his dream; *upon the path of each and every one of us, there is a snake waiting in ambush.*

As little Pulco dreamed at Phosphor's feet, Fantasma's sandbank dissolved like a magic dust beneath him. His servants were roused by his screams: he was no swimmer. They fished him out and propped him up in a dry corner of the wood against a stalwart tree free of ants. And they noted, with dismay, that a boil the size of a fig was flourishing at the tip of Fantasma's nose. When this was brought to Fantasma's attention, he began to curse, damning the world and his own mother who—without his consent—had precipitated him into it.

"It's not a bell chiming!" Phosphor, out of temper, handed him his gruel. Not used to being taken lightly, Fantasma thrust the bowl from him angrily.

"You don't understand!" he cried. "It wasn't there yesterday!"

"A mole," Phosphor insisted. "A speck of transitory and inconsequential matter."

"*Everything* is of consequence," Fantasma countered. "Fogginius said it again and again. I suffer his loss acutely." Fantasma struck his brow with his fist. "He could have told me if this was a malignancy or—despite my fears—a *felicity*."

The poet took a closer look and conceded that the thing was nasty; in a quiet way, it appeared to seethe.

"A pestilence!" Fantasma stroked it with tenderness and loathing, "at the center of my face. A plot! Perpetrated by lepers and Jews!"

"Practice the virtues of patience and hope." Phosphor imitated his stepfather's unctuous tones.

"The saint would have had a cure." Fantasma groaned. "The saliva of a virgin. A whore's intimate fluids. An innocent's blood. I wish I knew what!"

"I know his cure," Phosphor said: "A cataplasm of fermented sheep dung to be endured six times daily for sixty days and sixty nights." The bleb on Fantasma's nose visibly darkened.

"I will not forget this impertinence," said Fantasma. The quarrel ended in a noxious silence.

Starved and weary, the party arrived at Pope Publius in the middle of an afternoon so wretchedly hot the entire population was fast asleep in the deep cool of bedchambers tiled and shuttered, or open to shaded gardens where cool fountains played, filling the air with a chill vapor.

Despite the heat, little Pulco was cold with terror. He dawdled behind because he knew that if Fantasma's house had persisted in its absence, he would be surely beaten; he had noticed months before that whenever anything went wrong, he was the one who was blamed.

And horribly, when they came to the abandoned gate, with its angels and warriors of yellow brass parading across its length, the Big House studded with precious windows of Venetian glass and bristling with balconies was irretrievably gone. Fantasma's jaw dropped, the yellow bucket of a tooth dangling and trembling in the wind of his astonishment.

Life in the wild had taken its toll and it was at this precise instant that Pulco and Phosphor saw how Fantasma had diminished in breadth and height, as if all the while he had raved and rode and slept and stormed, Time had sucked the living marrow from his bones.

Recovering enough to move, Fantasma grabbed Pulco by the ear and began to thrash him. For a time, Phosphor was himself too flabbergasted to intervene, but stood gaping, wonderingly. He supposed there was a logical reason for the vanishment of so much substance, and he looked eagerly about him, expecting to see clues in the hills beyond. The sun continued to blaze in the sky—there was consolation—and the ground seemed solid enough. He considered, for the first time in his life, the possibility of miracles. But then he pulled himself together and searched the ground. Beneath a clump of flowering vine he found a broken chair, smashed crockery, and a key. As he meditated upon the vanity of things, he heard Señor Fantasma cry out in pain: Pulco had kicked him in the face and the last remaining relics of a once profusely furnished mouth had bit the dust. Without his teeth, Fantasma looked very like Fogginius. Dazed, Fantasma backed off and—lurching, a puppet on strings—began the hopeless task of discovering his house's whereabouts. ·

For a time, Phosphor and Pulco watched him running in ever widening and erratic circles; then they mounted their mules and took themselves to the public baths and the tailor's. Nuño Alfa y Omega intended to make a splendid impression when he stood upon the Tardanza threshold with a garland of blossoms the size of a lunar halo.

24

Before entering into this, my twenty-fourth chapter, it occurred to me, dearest Ved—you who have so often relished the pleasures of the island's bountiful tables— to order a meal for myself. To inspire and inspirit me, I selected a luncheon of shellfish from the House of the Edible Ark Clam's noontime menu.

Ah! The delights of the thorny oyster, the tender reproductive organs of the sea urchin palpitating in their bristling cuirass! The evocative architecture of tritons, the flesh within the gaping aperture softened with lime juice and sweetened with fragrant herbs! A toast, dearest friend, to the molluscan universe! Let us recall that in the aborigine cosmology, the first parent was the saffron-colored hermaphrodite island scallop!

The island scallop is unlike any other I know, and more than one scholarly monograph has been devoted to it. Thorned with scarlet spines, the twelve convergent ribs are a creamy salmon color, and the inner walls a luminescent purple. Its flesh is incredibly sweet, delicate, and tender. This afternoon I was regaled by a feast in the native manner: a cold dish of crabs lightly cooked in palm oil and flavored with lime juice, red pepper paste, and freshly ground coriander; a scallop soup containing coconut milk, ginger, lemongrass, and fresh basil; spitted scallop and thimble-sized chunks of spiny lobster roasted over embers and served with a hot red pepper sauce well-flavored with crushed cashews, peanuts, and herbs.

Like so many aspects of aboriginal culture, the island cooking has refused to die. And it seems to me that despite the fact that the Ancient Ones have vanished, Birdland's pulse is ever an erotic pulse quickened by appetite. Is it surprising that the feminine shell and phallic beak continue to be featured emblems on the national flag?

As if reading my mind, a lovely young woman who sat alone across the room devouring a platter of heart-shaped lunules raised her eyes to mine. The nature of her glance could not be misinterpreted. (The Ancient Ones believed that the capacity to look into another's eyes and read her mind is sorcerous.) And her eyes—their slow-burning quality, their depth and intensity—revealed something else: her aborigine ancestry.

The Ancient Ones, it was said, were all wizards: *shape-changers*. Gazing back into the enchanting stranger's eyes, 1 perceived a fleeting bestiary and recalled that the Old Fantasma had named one of his slaves Subtill Shift because he was a *changeling*. The thought came to me: perhaps I am in the presence of one of Subtill Shift's descendants! Shyly, I bit into a scallop and, to give myself courage, recalled Nuño Alfa y Omega's great lines:

> . . . *her eyes are moons; they orbit my soul*
> *two lunar fish transforming.*
> *They dart within the recesses of my bones.*

Her eyes are the forests I explore
in those hours when the universe contracts
to one lucent pearl of desire.

As I set to paper these impressions—the fruits of my researches in the shape of a romance—I realize that what the poet did with so much brilliance was to seize upon and illuminate the fearless delight in the sensory world informing aboriginal life, a joyous attitude born of the conviction that the transitory world, *ceaselessly renewed,* is eternal.

"There is no Heaven," the last great chief informed his persecutors before he died, "only this one life. It is a fire rekindled each time lovers embrace with hunger."

Those artifacts the latter-day Inquisitors would destroy—which, for example, show the Primal Mother fornicating turn by turn with pelicans, parrots, and porpoises—serve to illustrate the infinite aspects of the cosmic dance. One need only look at them with open eyes to see that these lyrical objects are not "abominable visions and abject hallucinations" (Rais Secundo) or "works of obscene and unhealthful minds" (The Clean Sweepers) but revelations of cosmic unity. Writes the poet:

Arboreal, aerial goddess
riding the phallic beaks of toucans;
goddess of the waters
copulating with clams; squid woman
daughter of the sacred scallop sheathed in
your codpiece of shell
more lovely than the miters of popes
the bloody crosses, the insipid wafers
of popes . . .

(And there you have the lines that damned him!)

"The aborigine," Secundo wrote, "hath no word for *chastity, abstinence, pudicity, indecency*, and yet hath sixty-nine words for *fornication*." This officer of the Inquisition is remembered for an extensive treatise—over 900 pages long!—on buggery in the islands entitled *One Thousand and One Beastly Practices of the Aborigines of Birdland and the Other Countries of the Favored Isles That Have Greatly Offended This Inquisitor*.

And—because he had read of the marvel in a book written by a bishop who feared fornication as much as he, Secundo was notorious for wearing a paper cone on his head. Upon it he had inked an emblematic fist giving the Devil the finger!

Notice his use of the present tense: for Secundo, the Ancient Ones were still very much alive. Furthermore, he admits to uncontrollable laughter whenever he sees an erotic bas relief, a scrap of painted pottery, a piece of perforated shell.

You are aware the Ancient Ones took a singular pleasure in the cigar. *They*, Secundo snorts, *hath no knowledge of the wheel but are the inventors of a grass nipple or teat upon with they chew. To see them set the end on fire and sucke the smoake is terrible to behold. When they sucke they look like devills: They says the smoak is magick, and with it mayke coniurations, negromancy spells, and fetche shaddowes.*

Again, Phosphor sets thing straight when he informs us that at the beginning of the world, the goddess, smoking and daydreaming, produced a seminal vapor. Rising in the air, it rose to the heavens and caused the Milky Way.

As you know, the waters of Oddingselle Bay are wonderfully transparent. Sitting on a stony lip of land one can peer down into the sea and perceive wonders as in a magic glass. The phenomenon was appreciated by the ancients who, at times of the full moon, from January to June, would come here to watch the tumultuous encounters of the mature island scallop—broken free of its byssal anchors—and the starfish. The lôplôp too would gather, for on such occasions a truce reigned between humankind and feathered beast; on summer nights of celestial brilliance, the lôplôp was not hunted.

When the scallop sees or senses the approach of the starfish, it makes a face—sucking in water before clapping its shell valves together and propelling itself with commotion and noise out of harm's way. Should a shell fall onto its back, it will somersault—a thing that caused much hilarity among the aborigines, and intense sexual arousal among the birds. Although this is a set piece entertainment, the clownish scallops and fatal stars as static in their roles as stage machinery, the choreography is irresistibly erotic.

It is here, to this rocky ledge, that I came with the lovely stranger on our first evening together. The moon was so swollen and so low that we were able to see the struggle clearly. When a scallop leapt out of the path of a prowling star and into the mortal embrace of another, Polly—yes! You had guessed it was she!—held her breath. As did I. And when the starfish coaxed the scallop's valves apart, we exhaled simultaneously and turned to one another. I felt my byssal anchors snap as for the first time those salmon-colored lips parted and I tasted of Polly's surprisingly cool and salty tongue. Ved: I am lost. *Irretrievably*. Rather, I am *found!*

25

When he looked back upon it, it seemed to Phosphor that his marriage had taken place in a dream. The instant he arrived at his intended's door, Professor Tardanza, perpendicular and shrill, and his silent, rhombohedral wife, swept him up in precipitous plans. For one brief hour he had encountered his beloved, in lace and cuneiform, flanked by her mother and an equally architectonic aunt. The procedures were all so terrifying that the poet, reduced to gumbo, stayed in the shadow of the event—even after it was over. Before he could blink, before he had time to awaken and find the legs with which to run, he was cornered by the priest and propped beside an unknown cipher metamorphosed into a heap of clothes.

The cathedral floor was paved with black and red tiles forming a labyrinth; concentric circles like ruptured intestines formed a visceral pathway. Staring at it, Phosphor felt dizzy and numb. The circular maze might be a wheel, the wheel of a mill. The poet thought: *I shall be ground to dust.* He imagined himself atomized and lifted into the air, to settle on someone's coat only to be brushed off with a careless gesture of the hand. He thought:

Man is but a ~~transient~~ stuff . . . a ~~sidereal~~ powder . . . on the ~~breath~~ . . . wind of ~~eternity~~ . . . finitude.

To add to the event's strangeness, a hideous baying, as of wolves, could be heard from time to time circling the cathedral. It was Señor Fantasma, mourning his vanished house. Near dawn, far from town, a scream of rage and pain shattered the air; propulsed by who knows what demons, Fantasma had sliced off his nose.

Throughout the wedding feast, Phosphor was haunted by hallucinations. His bride was a curiously shaped magnet and he a shaving of iron hopelessly caught at her side. A pig had been roasted entire, and Phosphor, having received its face for his portion as was customary, was overcome by an impression of being pushed headfirst into a pit. What was worse: when he dared steal a glimpse of his bride's face, he did not recognize her. *People*, he mused, *have a way of looking very unlike themselves up close.* He shuddered to think that he would be seeing her closer.

Pulco had said that she was beautiful. But the boy was illiterate and knew not the first thing about beauty. Phosphor hoped she was not all that beautiful: it was one thing to write beautifully, or to write about beauty, even beautifully—but to embrace it, alone in a darkened room, no! No! That was something else altogether. To *satisfy* beauty! That was, surely, beyond his capacities. Another glimpse. . . .

It *was* a beautiful face and yet meant nothing to him, despite his dreams, his longing in the woods to kiss it, lingeringly, on the lips. Of course, he did not know her, whatsoever. The poet considered this with a spark of hope. Not because, Heaven help him, it was a face devoid of meaning. He looked at it again. Extravaganza ate with appetite. Her own portion—the pig's tail, roasted to a turn—was between her faultless teeth reduced in minutes to a bone heap.*

When the feast was over, Professor Tardanza took his son-in-law by the elbow and together they paced the garden, presumably to give Extravaganza the time she needed to wipe the grease from her lips and to bathe her succulent body in a water scented by gardenias.

In the center of the garden was a pool and a little marble bench. Here the two men sat, Tardanza yawning but jocular, Phosphor agitated and depressed. He stared into that still water illumined by the moon, and for a brief moment considered drowning himself. It was then that something extraordinary happened:

Within the water, Phosphor saw a pair of eyes that—or so it seemed—expressed all those fugitive ideas he had been grappling with, not always successfully. The eyes opened out upon infinity, and eternity too. They seemed wise to him, and sweet. The poet's heart leapt up with recognition and delight. This time he was in love; he looked deeply into his beloved's eyes and did not falter; he did not see death, nor vortices, nor abysses; he saw limitlessness.

"That," said Professor Tardanza, pointing to the great copper-colored face just now breaking the surface, "is Extravaganza's pet carp." Reaching into a pocket he threw the fish a crust. "I shall be turning in." Tardanza patted the poet's back. "Extravaganza is waiting for you."

But Phosphor was lost in thought, lost in the contemplation of a creature so graceful, so coolly ethereal, he

---

* More from Ombos: *In the bed of the ogress, appetite, copulation, birth, death, and defecation are all contained in (and exemplified by) the vortex—and I use that word precisely because it best describes the vertiginous quality of Nuño Alfa y Omega's vision, as well as Jonathan Swift's. Swift's own vision was surely informed by his chronic malaise. Ménière's disease is best characterized by precipitous vertigo and severe unbalance. The world, in seizure, appears to spin.*

wondered: *Had it an anatomy? A spine? Had it ribs?* He imagined that only a creature *without feet* could be capable of transcendence. The fish was a vivid thing, languid and lovely—more syllable than animal; a tracery, and, as it flitted in and out the shadows, a thing of light.

He passed the night there, enraptured, perched upon the marble bench, tossing lumps of wedding cake to the fish.

Ved, before you look too long upon Phosphor's voluptuous fever (all the more so because it cannot be consummated), you must know that, at least for now, his bride Extravaganza, gorgeous vessel that she may be, does not miss him. As her groom sits dreaming and kneading crumbs into pellets, she is thinking about dolls' clothes.

She is an innocent creature, her one immodest act—performed for Pulco's benefit—in compliance with her father's wishes. Never has she entertained impure thoughts; she is, or so it seems, incapable of thought. (In Ombos's words: *It is sexual love that liberates the libido and sets the lover to dreaming. And so, becoming. . . .*) Often, to reassure her mother as well as himself, Tardanza had said of her:

"As Extravaganza is incapable of learning anything, she will never learn anything *dangerous*."

"She has the sweetness of the dumb creatures," the priest who has married her agrees: "Without one hairline fracture, her soul is as clean as any fish living in water, the very air it breathes well washed with water, its thoughts, water."

Perhaps, had he perceived her thus, Phosphor might have loved his bride with the same unreasoning enthusiasm he now demonstrates for her pet carp. But there is more:

As the poet meditated upon the resemblances and dissemblances of all things—how, for example, a lamb's rump

could be mistaken for a head of cauliflower—it came to him
that the human heart is very like the sea anemone pulsing
in saltwater, and how it was only natural that he should be
enamored of a creature making her home in water.

The little scales upon the fish's back were reflecting surfaces, an infinite array of small mirrors, so that if the light
was right, the poet could see his own eye gazing back at him,
or even his own face miniaturized and multiplied.

Days later, as Phosphor continued to spy upon the fish, a
large white slug fell into the pool and Phosphor was shocked
to see his beloved snap it up as eagerly as she did the bits of
cake he proffered so lovingly.

This phenomenon happened then: the poet recognized
the carp's corporeality *and his own.* His reflection reminded
him that he too ate to live. Phosphor had eaten squid for
supper, redolent of coconut milk and ginger. When the fish
excreted a surprisingly thick string of filth, the poet, shocked
again, was forced to reflect upon physicality and to accept
the nature of the world in its entirety.

His beloved, so like polished metal, so languid and signif-
icant, more the stunning consonant of some divine alphabet, more scroll than living creature—

So like fire, so silent, so entire, so entirely *other,* so con-
summately mysterious—was, as was he, bound by natural
laws. Why hadn't he realized this sooner? It was absurd, he
decided, laughing at his own folly, to expect that his beloved
be immaterial. Had she been so, he could not have adored
her as he did. As much as her vital corporeality, her mortal-
ity moved him. She was precious, he realized, because she
was not eternal, but an instant of delight to be seized before
eternal night would snap her up forever, snap them both up,
man and maid, forever.

Yet, just as this new idea came to him, two things happened simultaneously, and this for the poet's felicity:

First he recognized the absurdity of referring to a fish as a
maid; next, the image of Extravaganza appeared before him.
He rubbed his eyes and saw that she was truly there; indeed,
her perfume of fruit and flowers filled the air. Reflected in
the pool, her face wavered before him: curious, attentive, tender. Turning to her, and for the first time taking her hand in
his, Phosphor noted that she too palpitated with eager life.
He saw the blood pulse at her neck and was moved; saw the
sweetness within her eyes, her slender ribs, her hands like little
wings, her skin like hot sand. So acute was his vision that he
could see her unique vibrancy. The poet's bride had, in these
brief moments, eclipsed her rival, the fish.

I suppose, or I imagine, that it was then that Phosphor
realized—oh, not with his rational mind, but with his
soul—that words are the vehicles of meaning and intention,
not *things* to be sent buzzing in the void in order to fill it
with a digressive, numbing hum, but particles of meaning,
interactive and necessary. Now that Phosphor was ready to
love, he was also ready to speak *and so to write*—or so, dear
Ved, that is how I have come to see it. Because from that
night on, Phosphor's poems are no longer so much hot air
but the sails that—tugged this way and that by intuition—
set the little boats of life on course: swift, bright, and sure.
Guided by love, informed by desire, the vision incandesces
and the poems catch fire:

> *Extravagant,*[*] *the afternoon hums in your throat*
> *A palpable orbit in a sky of smoke*
> *Your face as necessary as the orbits of stars*

---

[*] Again, Ombos: *I find the pun on the poet's wife's name especially charming.*

The elusive, the essential trace of the sun.
You are the fire that tempers worlds
A rain of smoke, a planet of smoke.
You are the moon riding the scales of a carp in a pool
of light. The evening. The eye of the owl.

Written in an ink of flowers
Your voice is a sunlit stairway
Suddenly tangible in the wet morning.
Your voice is a rain, a fistful of petals
A serpent uncoiled in the sun.
Your voice is a fountain, the blood of plants, other
Precious things.

26

The poet and his bride retired to a secluded corner of the garden. The moon was hornless, and Extravaganza eager. At mass a week earlier, she had caught a glimpse of two lovers crouching behind an immense black basin of holy water, greedily kissing. Seeing this, however furtively, she had felt a drunken fire strike her womb. As the lovers gnawed at each other's lips, her own teeth ached, and the dark room, smelling of candle grease and unwashed choirboys, now smelled of limes and freshly husked oysters—the astonishing scent of her own desire.

It was then that Extravaganza wondered why her wedded state was so very like the other—indeed, her life was unchanged, the only difference being that a large bed had replaced the small one of her infancy, and that she no longer slept alone. Although she might as well have—for the poet crept in beside her long after she had fallen into a deep, dreamless void. Sleep claimed her until morning when the downstairs maid, bristling with ill temper, roused them both for breakfast by rattling crockery and stomping on the floor.

Shyly, after mass, Extravaganza had asked her mother what it was that brought men and women together, and

what obscure acts were performed when they were alone—
was it a species of worship? And were children really cunningly fashioned sugarloaves brought to life by a bishop in a
bakery—as she had been taught—or was the mystery of ori-
gins somehow far more marvelous? But her mother would
not answer, and growing darker, collapsed deeper into the
rhomboidal impenetrability that characterized her even on
the best of days. It was the cook who, in no uncertain terms,
laid it all out before her in the shape of stories plebian and
poetical altogether, stories of her own courtship, the love
affairs of all her friends; she described in detail everything
Extravaganza could, *should* expect of her young husband.
That night Extravaganza reread the poet's letters, and this
time burned—for certain allusions, unintentional perhaps,
but born of the author's own secret desires, were now clear.

As it turned out, Extravaganza was not so much dumb
as untried, and that long evening alone with the letters, and
the vital vision of the numinous kiss she had seen, awakened
an inexorable longing. It dissipated the vague veil hanging
over her mind, clouding that organ and weakening it; a
longing that informed and animated her soul ever after.

Until then, Extravaganza had been submerged in the
sugar icing of a tradition ruinous to the clairvoyance of
girls; she had been, like so many of her kind, purposely
benumbed. Her tutor, Enrique Saladrigas, had taught her
to read both Latin and Spanish, but her own mother had
forbidden her access to her father's library. (Saladrigas had
been sent packing the very day Phosphor saw him and his
beloved riding together—for having had the good sense to
tell the girl that the eggs of birds are not put into nests by
the hand of the infant Jesus.)

If Extravaganza's mother—little more than an amorphous

lump given form and substance by corsets—could do nothing for her, her father dared not do too much. In some listing chamber of his soul he feared that a curious child, a fearless child, might one day question his authority. Nevertheless, it greatly distressed him that no one in his family dreamed. Tardanza was troubled by an inkling that he and his family were monstrous somehow, their inability unforgivable. Secretly he delved into the sacred books of the cabala and they informed his worst fears: *An unacknowledged dream is an unopened letter.* He had taken to sleeping with his feet in a tub of chopped liver.

That night in the garden, Phosphor proved a potent lover, solicitous and tender. The famished virgin's sweet embrace brought to mind new honey, freshly baked bread, the ocean summer storms, deep-sea diving, mango harvests, soft-boiled eggs, caviar, pears cooked in wine, black earth, salted herring, vanilla, blossoming nasturtiums, avocados, and the velvet of new antlers. Phosphor forgot himself entirely, forgot his history, forgot the world and thought only of climbing that enchanted precipice of barely cool lava, new moss, and sea foam leading to a pulsing, ovular star burning with such intensity that he kept his eyes tightly shut all the while—else be blinded. Just as he reached that star and seized it hungrily with both his fists, Extravaganza cried out in a voice so altered and arcane his heart was lost, recovered in its entirety, and lost again—this time irretrievably. And as that cry reverberated for an instant in their corner of the spinning world, the moon, illumined by the eye of love, shone brighter, leaving in its wake a fleece of clouds. Beneath those clouds, intertwined, both Phosphor and his bride were already dreaming. So that the next morning at breakfast, Extravaganza, twigs in her hair and her head as cluttered as any collector's cabinet, could say: "Father! I have dreamed!"

It was true that Extravaganza was somehow transformed. Her father looked at her, perhaps for the first time, with curiosity. But when he asked her to describe her dream, she could only blush and shake her head. You will not be surprised to learn that she had dreamed of love.

"My dream is *mine*, Papa," she said, her face strangely diffused with a lunar light; "I cannot share it with anyone." And the poet—had he dreamed as well? He had: a dream of a sexual extravagance so acute he was, as he recalled it now, still shaken. He had dreamed of his own member; dreamed that it had grown the size of a large man, a royal personage sporting a great candy crown of sugarplums and spun sugar; that this phallus-person had stood before him and, bowing, *introduced himself.*

"I dreamed of candy," the poet said, "and about a king. I cannot recall the rest."

❧

Dearest Ved—Having now read all of the poet's vast opus, I can with certitude say this: When Phosphor made love to Extravaganza, the vortex of his cowardice, the gaping maw of his alarm vanished, and it was as if he had come into the world fearless, staff in hand. In Extravaganza's arms, his torment was melted down and reduced to a sweet honey that she extracted fearlessly. Her tender body gave itself utterly and unabashedly; being simple and having no notion of evil, she was an Edenic animal seized by heat. Her eyes and cunt wept with happiness; her breasts filled the poet's mouth like those magical fruits that are renewed as they are eaten. The feast was an eternal feast, or so it seemed, and the nights they spent together, all too swiftly done, somehow sprawled into infinity, abolishing not only terror but self and time.

Because it seemed to Extravaganza that, in the poet's embrace, her body dissolved and reorganized into infinite series of animate and inanimate things—sea urchins and clamshell rattles, ivory clappers, ferns and fishskin drums— once she had surfaced from the oceans, lakes, burrows, nests, marshes, mud, sand pits, oyster-beds, and whirlpools of love, she battled bewilderment, unsure of where she was and, for that matter, *what* she was. Standing stark naked and quivering before her mirror, and slapping her sweet ass with her open palms, she would cry, as if surprised: "I am a human female!"

The poet entered into a loving and living dream; it claimed him, even when awake. All day long Phosphor was haunted by the nights, which, as the seasons progressed, hung strung together like amber beads on a golden wire. These he gnawed and worried in his mind. Dazzled by love, Phosphor's cock and his heart had become one and the same animal.

These were blissful days and weeks—the most delightful of their lives. Phosphor, himself transformed, abandoned his epic—a pretentious and patriotic work—to devote himself to an inspired poetic revery on the nature of sensual love. Convinced that he had entered the secret chamber of an occulted mystery, he took it upon himself to reveal the prodigy to the vast world. His verse was a steaming milk, a wizard's ink—and it rained upon the page, page after page. As Extravaganza slept, or sucked a plum, or beside the open window combed her hair—which, free of ribbons, tumbled to her toes—Phosphor described in amorous detail love's multiplicitous vocabularies of salutations and smiling receptions, overturning the natural realm in order to ambush the metaphorical creatures that would do desire justice; for example, *the Gazelle* (or *When the Beloved Attempts to Flee the Arrow*), *the Lion* (or *Embracing, the Lovers are Encircled by an Invisible Yet Palpable Mane of Fire*). And because he had not forgotten how a fish had unlocked his once solitary heart, Phosphor called his favorite embrace (although hard-pressed to name a favorite, as in bed with Extravaganza each act of love precipitated and included all the others)—that embrace during which the female, mounted from behind and knowing that the molten ring of her delight has moored her lover utterly, brings her thighs together as best she can, and the male, pushing his way in even deeper—as if that were possible—clutches his mistress' breasts to further anchor himself—this position the poet called *the Carp*.

After a convoluted correspondence with the university rector and the chief librarian, Phosphor was given permission to contemplate—in the company of a Consultant to the Holy Office of the Inquisition—an ancient manuscript from India proposing entire zodiacs of love in the shapes of copulating animals and mythic beings: blue gods and mortal women, black and white; red goddesses and mortal men, white and black. As the poet contemplated the book in a fever, the Consultant groaned and agitated his censer.

In the fragrant mornings, the garden ablaze with butterflies, parrots rioting in the trees, Phosphor would return to work:

My beloved's body is a delirious moon
A garden where foxes* paw and suck the grapes.
Her body is a vine plundered by foxes,
A tempest in a forest, a rain of black honey.
Her body is my darkness, total, luminous.
Her body is a rose of beaten gold;
It burns against my heart.

Extravaganza was dreaming and nothing could stop her; enchantment bubbled forth to inundate her soul with an effervescent water. Rather than eat breakfast, the lovers lay together until late, their tongues touching—and she would whisper the tumult of visions that, flooding the night, had submerged her. The poet listened to her eagerly, his cock throbbing between the buttocks of his beloved, his fingers lovingly investigating her wet fur.

Often, as she would describe some astonishing dream of thunderstorms and weirdly horned and pelted animals, or floating cities constructed of mother-of-pearl and brass, or harems wherein all the houris had the faces of ibises or tigresses, yet were in all their other parts human and sweetly formed, the poet would grasp his bride by the thighs and pull her to him. Compliant, already yielding, she would yield further, and for a time the telling of the dream would cease. Then, save for the sound of their breathing and the acute hammering of their blood, and the creaking and thudding of their windswept vessel, their chamber would fall silent.

Once, Extravaganza awoke wildly laughing. As she

---

* Says Ombos: *There are no foxes in Birdland. This is, evidently, a reference to Pliny.*

explained to Phosphor, in her dream she had seen the face of God. She recognized the nose at once—it was her lover's cock; the apples of His cheeks, Phosphor's balls. The Lord's beard, hairs upon hairs, curls upon curls, and the place from which He spoke and breathed the breath of life was her own splendid cunt.

27

Phosphor's delight in the world was at times troubled by a recurrent nightmare in which Fogginius was restored for the sole purpose of chewing off his stepson's ears, or worse: the ears of Poetry itself. Whenever he dreamed this, Phosphor gnashed his teeth with such ferocity that his jaw would ache and he constrained to sip tea and broths for forty-eight hours.

Extravaganza supposed the dreams served some purpose. "Even flies serve a purpose," she reasoned, "for by producing maggots they rid the refuse heaps of offal and dead cats which would otherwise infect the air."

"Maggots," the poet corrected her, "are engendered spontaneously in cheese."

"Flies drop seeds," Extravaganza insisted; "they, in turn, hatch maggots. These things have I, with patience, perceived. My eyesight is sharper than yours, dearest," she chided him (and this was so). Phosphor, having badly strained his eyes by writing deep into the night by candlelight, now wore a diminutive pair of spectacles hooked to the thin bridge of his nose, although his skin chafed easily.

"The dream is a warning of some kind," Extravaganza insisted. "You're the one with brains; you figure it out."

Now that Phosphor was both dreaming *and embracing a dreamer*, the world became a poem—that is to say, he no longer saw himself as one who translates the real into poetry, but one who transcribes the poetry of the real. "The universe," he whispered to his beloved in her embrace, "is a poem of love. The stars themselves are voluptuous inscriptions, as are the clouds, the salt water, the leaves. Each tree is a book of pleasures."

"Last night," Extravaganza suddenly recalled, "I dreamed you were the sky, my dearest, bowing over me. I was the earth, my breasts two hills, and my navel a sweet pool of fresh water. Your body was also a hive of honey; your body was tattooed with light."

This dream gave Phosphor his most celebrated line, the one that begins the section called "The Cosmological Suite" (Ombos' title):

> *Your body a zodiac tattooed with light*
> *Your body animated by a sweet flame*
> *Your body of translucence, your subtle body*
> *Raining starlight, always raining, raining honey.*

At times when Phosphor embraced Extravaganza, it seemed to him he held within his arms the four cardinal points, the four seasons, and the four winds.

"I dreamed," she said, after yet another night of love, "that I was Eve and you Adam, and that we were joined together by the flesh that grew over our hearts. God came and was ferocious-looking, like a lion and a snake combined;

He had the tail of a scorpion, and wings of fire. Seeing us thus joined together, our blood the same blood, our pulse one and the same, our thought one thought, He grew jealous and severed the bridge of flesh joining us with his sword. I saw that it was an ancient sword and had been used countless times.

"As you fell from me I cried out—so great was the pain in my heart. And, indeed, even now I feel a hurtful yearning—although I lie here beside you." The tender child began to weep in her lover's arms.

28

One night, very late, Phosphor and Professor Tardanza were engaged in feverish conversation. Enchanted by the ocular-scope, Professor Tardanza proposed to finance the machine of Fantasma's greed: large enough to hold one thousand and one slides—not for magical reasons, but because "Looking into it, or so I imagine, will be like dreaming," Tardanza said, and he continued thus: "The world is full of those who do not dream, who dream but do not remember, or whose dreams are not as beautiful as your images on glass. I know—I have spent my life recording the dreams of others. I think," he said solemnly, "we could simultaneously make a fortune and perform a great service for mankind—especially if the images could be *projected* somehow, much like a magic lantern show, and offered to crowds."

"And if . . ." Phosphor, in profound thought, gnawed his knuckles till they bled. "And if they could be made to move. *Truly* move. I'm not talking *clockworks* here." But Tardanza did not hear him. He was too busy pulling manuscripts from the shelves of his study; these shelves covered every wall from floor to ceiling and all were stuffed "to the gills," as he pointed out. Just as Phosphor had seized the island's visible aspect upon his glass plates, so Professor Tardanza had seized its reveries on parchment and paper. "It is surprising," Tardanza continued, "how eager most people are to describe their dreams. Many, it is true, are nightmares, and, I suppose, that in the telling my dreamers unburdened themselves.

"Here," Tardanza pulled a mauve, liver-spotted binding from a shelf, "are the dreams of a sixteen-year-old with the lovely name Eurasia. Eurasia dreams six times a night and always in blazing color. Should you like to take a look, you will see that her dreams are as incandescent, as frenetic, as volatile as hummingbirds. Last week, for example, she dreamed of a hole in the sky through which the eye of God was directly gazing, causing forests to ignite and the oceans to evaporate." He pulled down another book, this one scarlet and green.

"Here are the dreams of a very old man who, in his youth, was a brigand of the most ignoble sort. He captured the aborigines of an island off the coast of Hoppe Lumpe and sent them to Spain where they were exhibited in the palace gardens. A few were sold to the circuses, and others to the School of Medicine in Barcelona. One survived long enough to learn to express his anger with eloquence in the language of his captors. A noblewoman heard about the 'talking beast' and bought him. She kept him in her parlor, chained like a parrot to a perch and dressed in a skirt of grass designed by the chief seamstress to the Royal Opera. One day, in a rage, he broke free, throttled his tormentor, and vanished.

"The old man's dreams are always the same—with slight variations. He dreams in one color: a blackish red, the color, he says, of clotted blood. He dreams he awakens in his coffin, deep beneath the ground, and that the worms feasting upon his heart are his sole companions. Now, I am convinced that his dreams are his punishment, and I am certain there is a key here, a beautiful golden key to the human soul—but that key eludes me." He grabbed Phosphor's hand. "Marriage, son-in-law," he said, "has given my daughter an imagination. Last night she dreamed an empty throne suspended in midair; she dreamed she was a parrot flying above an infinite vista of mango trees. The fruit was ripe and its odor filled the air. That—and the sound of insects, wasps and bees—feeding on the fruit. Next she dreamed she wore a dress of pink camellias—"

"—and the dress," Phosphor finished the sentence for him, "was, in fact, a garden growing from her body."

"If I myself as yet do not know how to dream," Professor Tardanza continued, "I have numerous theories; for example, that dreams are exhalations of the divine—of Will, if you prefer, or of Infinite Capacity. In other words, an ecstatic vapor, the dust of Potencies, or even the inventions of the gods as they sit together swapping myths on their mountains. Somewhere I've written—" and he prodded through a pile of parchment in a cabinet "—that sleeping minds are the crystal balls of some other universe. Recently it came to me that sleep might be the theater where a sublunary race stages its plays; or even the playrooms of angels.

"But my favorite hypothesis (I do not believe in angels) is that dreams are the keys to the human soul—although it is true that this conjecture causes much merriment among my colleagues, and confusion among inquisitors."

"I am convinced this is so," said Phosphor, "for the theater of the world is played out within the human mind and the only gods and angels are those conjured by fools. And I am also convinced that the day I happen to make my pictures move I shall be tied to a post and burned for sorcery by those very same fools who, if they dream angels, dream devils too!"

"Some," Tardanza whispered, "have already been burned for less. But do not worry yourself," he added, patting the poet on the back, "pictures cannot be made to move."

These days in Professor Tardanza's house were the happiest little Pulco had ever known. He loved the house dearly, and Professor Tardanza, touched by the child's curiosity and his yearning for the beautiful, allowed him to wander the rooms freely, so that Pulco could be seen gazing an entire hour at a secretary painted with mysteriously gesturing figures, or shyly stroking the mahogany wings of the sphinxes that graced the arms of the dining room chairs. A large lacquered screen showed two griffins pulling a chariot full of winged children, and a set of small tables—turbaned figures dancing with tambourines.

The house, with its dream library, was itself a dream. On the parlor mantel were displayed twelve large birds of porcelain with painted feathers and gilded beaks. And, as we have seen, from every corner of the house trompe l'oeil winked; one hallway, its walls painted in false perspective, its ceiling tricked, appeared to be a full fifty feet long but was, in fact, under twenty. The door at its far end was so small, Pulco had to crawl into it on his hands and knees. He discovered that he had found the back door to Professor Tardanza's study.

The house bristled with lanterns, too, and Venetian candelabra blazed from dusk to midnight in the mirrors of every room. Tardanza taught Pulco to read; he had a theory that intelligence had nothing to do with social distinctions.

"The first letter, the aleph, is masculine," he explained to little Pulco; "it thrusts and prods with bluster, leads the alphabet forward, into the future. Beth, feminine and yielding, comes after—giving aleph courage to be. She is buxom: see her breasts!" And he drew a little picture:

"Together," Tardanza explained, "they engender all the letters that follow."

Pulco learned quickly. And because he was a profuse dreamer, began to fill his own dream book with dreams and also pictures of dreams and dream objects, and dream landscapes; the cities and forests and rivers of dreams.

Professor Tardanza also taught Pulco the secret craft of painting: how to achieve the translucency of shadow, for example, the opacity of light; how to render a pearl or an almond so realistically one would attempt to seize it; or a fly upon the lip of a vase; or a tear poised upon a cheek appearing to blush as one stared. (Not long ago, dear Ved, in that junk shop on Blue Parrot Street you so delighted in during your last visit, I discovered a miniature painted on gessoed wood. I like to think it was painted by little Pulco. It represents a lone, halved oyster shining wetly on a somewhat laboriously rendered pewter dish; the overall effect is mysterious and charming—and touching, too, for the painter is clearly a beginner. The signature is the single letter p, which could be a p (or v or j)—I let you be the judge!)

Entire days passed in a peaceful excitement: Pulco painting butterflies and lizards on the walls of all the rooms; Phosphor writing the verses that would make his forgotten island famous in the twentieth century and building his gigantic ocularscopic machine; Tardanza experimenting with new porridges and puddings to engender reveries; and Extravaganza roaming the garden and describing its riotous orchids and copulating dragonflies to the little child forming, instant by instant, in her womb.

However, this peace was badly disrupted when Señor Fantasma, more crazed than sane, and more dead than alive, arrived one late afternoon demanding asylum. After much discussion he was taken in—a perilous mistake. Awaking in clean linen sheets the following morning, Fantasma was convinced the house was his and the Tardanzas all interlopers. He pushed the little maids into corners and closets or threw himself upon them as they bent over the floor tiles with their soapy rags. Over dinner he argued absurd philosophical questions once raised by Fogginius in Fogginius' voice and with such dogmatic stridency everyone's guts knotted before they had tasted the soup. When once Fantasma ranted for a full hour on the voices of angels—"They have no balls and so have the voices of *castrata*"—he sounded so much like Fogginius that Phosphor found himself considering the possibility of transubstantiation.

The crisis came when Fantasma, suffering from cataracts as well as delusions, took Tardanza's wife to be a fat Venetian trollop he had known in his youth and whose specialty was producing vanilla-scented farts. He chased Señora Tardanza up the stairs, all the while brandishing a holy candle he had stolen from the family chapel.

Señora Tardanza stumbled into her husband's study screaming. Professor Tardanza owned a set of primate skulls (all on display in the museum and belonging to indigenous species now extinct). Her house guest hot upon her heels, Señora Tardanza slammed the study door behind her and pushed the bolt. Then, seeing the skulls staring at her from their shelf, she screamed again. Turning pink in her laces, she stood before her husband sobbing, as Fantasma hammered on the door spouting obscenities.

Out in the street within the half-hour, Fantasma, the tin nose securely in place, was led by the hand by Phosphor, who explained how he must turn the ocularscope's handle in such a way as to keep it from jamming—the first model was far from perfect—and how he must keep the machine clean from dust, and how he must take care to lock it up at the end of the day. Little Pulco brought up the rear with the ocularscope tottering dangerously before him in a large wheelbarrow. Fantasma was given a chair, a new pair of spectacles to protect his eyes from the sun, a box to keep his gainings in, and left to fend for himself on the east end of the market—the very same market that, even to this day, quickens the heart of the city.

From the first hour, long rows of Publians stood beneath the sun in order to peer into the ocularscope. And it seemed to them that here, indeed, the world had been seized as within the fist of God, and shrunk, and yet: these frozen instants, these particles of the real, evoked such powerful emotions that everyone who saw them knew they were magical.

When one had seen the backside of one's wife as she bent

over a bushel of guavas, that backside appeared in reality to have *diminished drastically*—as if the image captured on glass had more weight than the original. Which, in point of fact, it had, for long after a wife had moldered and atomized under the ground, her image, kept safely in a mahogany box along with so many other images of a lost world, would survive.

So that the ocularscope had this nefarious effect upon all the citizens of Birdland who turned its brass knob: from the time they had looked at their island and its population reduced to chemical powders and glass, the real seemed less real, and thus less precious. Until then transience was cherished for giving life its poignancy and meaning. Now that it could be kept filed away and retrieved at any moment, the real world seemed not only less real but also less desirable. For a few pennies one might gaze upon a naked beauty in her bath and thereafter desire that fictive being more than any real woman of flesh. The Inquisitorial Office was informed of the heresy. Fantasma was arrested for promulgating necromancy, as was Nuño Alfa y Omega, and the box was confiscated.

Rais Secundo examined the slides with a growing excitement. The images were profoundly seductive; for days altogether he gazed in terror and famishment at the vanished Cosima—with whom he was already intimate and who was now the talk of the town. And if he had previously been captivated by her in two dimensions, the ocularscope provided him with three. Thus was his pleasure and his pain expanded.

Secundo justified his fascination by choosing to consider his emissions as a purge, a temporary forfeiture of grace that caused him to dream constantly of hell. These dreams were a species of expiation. They provided him with the raw matter of prayers such as he had never before uttered, an inspiration and a fire he had never before known.

He looked upon his own intense excitement as a proof of sortilege: the more he gave in to it, the greater was the evidence of glamour. If the creature in the box was an illusion created by a puissant sorcerer, and his traffic with her not corporeal but virtual, the Inquisitor's own powers, now tested, were greater: his member did not dissolve as was customary in such cases. When, forgotten by all but for God, he, in his tower, admired its moonlit substantiality and compared it to the bell tower of a great cathedral, he recalled with a shudder the Church's unbounded influence over the transient world. And he recalled the poet's interest in the forbidden Eastern obscenities. After a brief investigation, Segundo learned that Phosphor had accompanied the heretic Fogginius and the madman Fantasma on a pilgrimage to the pagan sites in the aboriginal forest. Tardanza's house was searched, his dream materials were taken as well as Phosphor's manuscript, which was delivered to the Inquisitor, who sat upon a pewter *chaise percée* in a spare room with an impeccably mopped and polished floor.

The boxe and the poem, Secundo wrote in his report to the Spanish authorities, *doth procure illusory glamoures and cause combustion of the internal organs and uncleane dreams. Both are the devile's own repositories of seductions, powerful enow to seduce entire populations.*

As has been only recently revealed to the world, Phosphor had written a poem in which all the delights of the body, all those secret pleasures that unite the sexes in a lucent blindness—in fact *a way of seeing*—were not only listed by name, but described in loving detail.

He speakes, Secundo continued, *of gazing into his beloved's eyes where, juste as a sorcerer reads the future in bowls of quicksilver and in the palpitating viscera of slaine beastes, so doth he reade his destinie. He would have us believe that his beloved's part speakes to him in the voice of prophecy, that the moles upon her boddie form an alphabet, and the lines of her bellye map Paradise. He names love a transcendent magick and sayeth the lovers' boddies are the crucibles which transforme the soule.*

One daye, Secundo concludes his condemnation, *Satan shall be banished from the minds of men. The imagination crushed beneath the Pope's heel like the turd of a dogge. Then and only then will the world be scoured downe to the bone of Divine Justice and swept cleane. I dream of the daye when both the soules of men and the world will be as smoothe as a new piece of parchment so that a man coulde see to the world's four corners—see those four sacred regions, that exactly touch the celestial canopie. The Inquisitor, armed with a candle, will, by peering into the ears of men, see a perfect void. The labyrinth will be as foreign to the minde as the notion of dreaminge. Mankinde will procreate only from necessity. Luste and dreaminge, I have ascertained, are inexorably joined.*

29

My old friend Ved: this week a large number of carvings were unearthed in the biscuit-colored beach off Half Moon Reef. All those elements one has come to recognize as central to the aborigine cosmos are here: the lost lôplôp, the horned lizard, the laughing parrot so needlessly decimated by Fogginius. Vulture and bee (both princes of the air) are here, as are the spirit of wind, water, and weather. Coral and quartz are represented as beautiful women, as is fire. Touch, moonbeam, and starlight are children; decay, ashes, sight, and foresight are all fanciful beings, part man, part beast.

In the center of an orbit warped by telluric upheaval, the Master and Mistress of Cosmic Things were found deeply buried and tenderly entwined. With the fingers of his right hand, he, even now, gently presses his beloved's nipple; spurting milk, it will create the Caribbean Sea. Throbbing and thrashing in her fist, his sex is about to inseminate the waters.

Because of the significance of the find, the island is making ready to receive prominent cosmologists from the world over. I sincerely hope—despite the dubious intelligence that you are, as you say, "getting quite old, too old, my wife insists, for fantasy"—that you, beloved teacher and friend, will be among them.

The Clean Sweepers, torn asunder by patriotism and their hatred of the sensual world and its sexual determinisms, are hotly debating among themselves. There has been a renewed interest in the museum and its collections.

Today, when I returned, it thundered and squalled with schoolchildren. I had not seen it so animated in years. Protected by the newly installed electronic eye, the island Venus stood in all her luminous beauty—the light streaming through the rotunda's glass dome was especially bright. I turned left into the west wing and, clearing a sweeping run of marble steps, passed through the hall that bristles with the gigantic skeleton of a whale. (It is said that at the time of the conquest, they swam the environs of the island in such numbers it was difficult for lesser vessels to navigate safely.)

There is a curiously tenacious story—perhaps you have heard it?—that the island was once peopled by a race of giants who fed upon whales just as you and I feed upon whiting. As if, with time, the whimsical pygmies of the conquest—living in baskets and chewing cigars—had become as big as their own cosmology, as gigantic as the harm done to them. A preposterously somber oil painting of the Old Fantasma, wearing a blood-splattered cloak and a ruff of sea silk, lords over this ordered boneyard.

A passing comment on the tyrant's collar: the aborigine harvested the byssal filaments of a narrow shell genus *Pinna*, which once proliferated in the region. These threads were woven into a sumptuous cloth they used for bedding. The secret of Birdland's own golden fleece, was lost when the last native weaver died refusing to reveal the sacred place where the *Pinna* were harvested. The supremely rare collar illumines a bitter face, umbrageous and cruel.

Of the silk, not a fragment remains. The collar—for a time displayed beneath a glass bell—succumbed, despite precautions, to the larva of a moth coincidentally named *Argonautae* by the island's own celebrated lepidopterist (I believe you have met him): Professor Capricornes (now ninety!).

Back to the *récit* of my morning. Referring to a map hastily sketched in an acutely feminine hand in sepia ink on the back of a used envelope, I entered into a maze of rooms previously unknown to me, passed the laboratory of fossil vertebrates (a surprising amount of sawing and hammering came from within and the hallway was hazy with dust, so assiduously were the remains of extinct species being coaxed from their prisons of limestone and shell). Taking the stairs and turning left, I passed through the storage of mammals—a queer room of oiled shelvings and cabinets crowned with rows of skulls. Then down a corridor of specimens kept in alcohol—the soft shell-less bodies of volutes, conches, and cones for the most part—or so I was informed by their labels.

Finally, circuiting the dome of the amphitheater and ascending a stairwell that leads to a tower, I entered the room of marine invertebrates, a charming room painted an uncharacteristic butter yellow, and illumined by one graceful arched window overlooking the kindly trees of the botanical gardens. Here is a room packed like a cornucopia with wonderfully named shells: tulips and spindles, nanunculi and lilliputs, lyrias and music volutes, torrids and lion's paws, combs of Venus, mice, ladders, turbans, olives, and apples! And here I found the rarest lion's paw of all—Polly with her tangled hair, hazel eyes, and little round spectacles.

Polly had spent the morning painting a series of unique moon shells (she and Professor Cocles—Rojo, yes! He is still full of vim and vinegar!—are compiling a definitive work on the subject). She had rendered them in full color in relief with such conviction that *I attempted to pick one up!*

"*You smell of ambergris,*" I said to her, touching her neck with my lips and quoting Nuño Alfa y Omega's poem: "*my love, you smell of almonds.*" We kissed for one long moment and Polly, who knows the poem now as well as I (in fact one cannot go anywhere on the island these days without hearing its verses, which have all been put to music), replied:

"*Your fragrance is the fragrance of morning.*"

Indeed, Phosphor's poem, transmuted into the stuff of twentieth-century romance by the rhythms of a Birdland-style bolero, filtered up to us from the street below:

> *. . . of those mornings when*
> *searching for shells I find treasure*
> *a book of water written in an ink of salt.*
> *And your taste is the taste of tempest*
> *of those stormy hours when the wind, unbound,*
> *tastes of foam; when the stars, unfixed,*
> *taste of sleep; when the visible sea tastes of love.*
> *You are all the seasons, all the hours*
> *every kind of weather*
> *all the minutes of fleeting time.*
> *My protean dancer, my fish, my panther*
> *You taste of water*
> *and your taste is the taste of a dream*
> *from which I awaken transformed.*

Polly had acquired for me the key to the museum's darkest collection—those objects used by the Inquisition to break the bones and the spirits of its enemies. I wanted to see the funnel that had served to pour quicklime down the poet's throat. I wanted to hold it in my hand so that I could never forget such a thing had happened: that a poet had been silenced simply because he had been passionately in love. And I wanted to confront the obscene funnel armed with the knowledge that the poet had not been silenced after all; that his poem (discovered just a few steps from Polly's laboratory) had not only survived—it was flourishing.

In fact, the funnel was forgotten. For as she proffered the key, Polly had, with a glance and an affectionate gesture, expressed her longing for me. And so within that room of scattered sunlight and sumptuous shells, we set about to participate in the ancient dance—I might say *the one dance and the only dance that matters* and that is so beautifully represented by both Phosphor's poem and those aboriginal carvings of couplings so recently brought to light.

Ved, I know you will ask further precisions concerning the stone figures. My first impulse will be to say: *Come!* Come at once and see them for yourself! And while you are at it, come feast your eyes upon my beloved too; come witness our affection and be embraced by its festive warmth! We shall celebrate our amorous encounter *next month*. Come for the feast! Twelve sorts of oysters (Polly and I will have known one another twelve weeks), twelve sorts of scallops and clams, twelve sorts of mussels, champagne, and lime pie!

I have just viewed the figures myself—all mossy and

caked with deposits of clay and sand (and the little egg-sacks of spiders and rootlets of ferns and the small bones of lizards . . .). I cannot contain my excitement. For these are clearly elemental powers, those potent inventions that informed the aboriginal universe with a poetic intention. What is more, each has a text inscribed at its base: the aborigines, despite the historians' insistence to the contrary, had a written language and a sumptuous alphabet that the prominent scholar Gertrude Hubble regards as a syllabary containing forty consonants (many of these are clicks), the vowel sounds implied, perhaps, by the number of hairs or horns or spots or stripes or teeth or eyes or petals or tongues appearing on letters for the most part in the shapes of creatures: snake, snail, starfish, etc. The text at the base of the spine of one great basaltic torso looks a little like this (I never was an artist!) and is read, according to Hubble, from top to bottom, left to right:

Rumor has it that Hubble has cracked the code, and we await her revelations breathlessly. (All the more reason for you to come!) Thus far she has, in private, divulged only this to me:

t'k   : turtle
       half moon
       empty bowl

t'kk! : turtle-moon rising
       from the sea
       (or: the birth of an idea)

w'tk! : turtle moon rising across horizon
t'kk   (or: the extension of an idea)
       (Also: festival week: moving from
       one place to another)

w'h   : full bowl of turtle soup
t'ka   (auspicious event)

Dear friend! This morning I awoke laughing. I had been dreaming of days past and a thing you once said surfaced in my dream. You recall, I am certain, those conversations that so engaged us in the late seventies when, far away in Colorado, a brilliant (and heretical!) natural historian suggested (or rather, revealed) that the dinosaurs were fleet, smart, and colorful. "And not," you said, "*grey*—as we had been taught—as though the great lizards were nothing more than the discarded plumbing of the Industrial Revolution!"

Last night, alone with my beloved on the black sands of Point Comfort Beds, I gazed upon the zodiacs peculiar to my island's particular neck of the woods. And it seemed to me that forming distinctly above my head was the outline of a female figure, full-bodied and on her hands and knees. And that pulsing behind her, close upon the twin orbs of her bountiful posterior, kneeled a great beaked figure—an enigmatic lôplôp. . . .

FROM POLLY'S SKETCHBOOK

Mostly of uncertain Phage
Cache 2 · Barren Bottoms

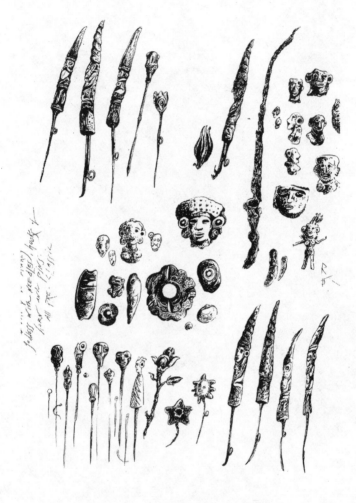

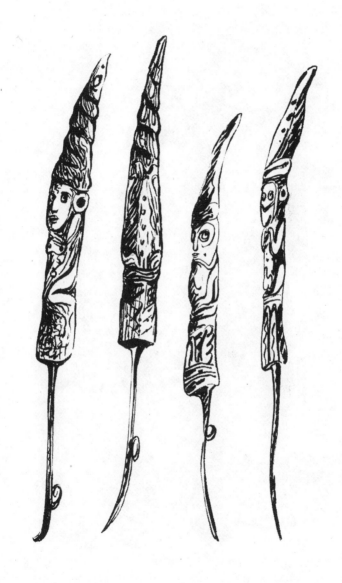

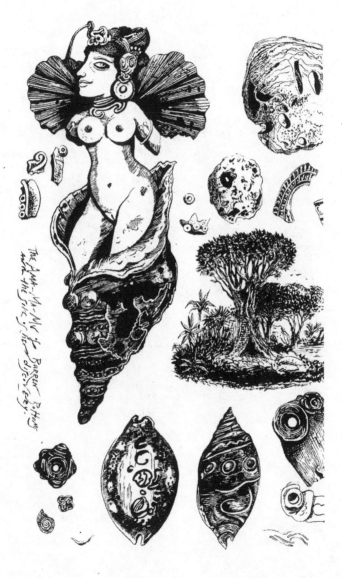